The Legend of Dynamite George

The Mining Pack Rat

CARROLL BENNETT

Published by Foto Fantasi Press
www.dynamitegeorge.com
packrat@dynamitegeorge.com

through

Winmark Communications
17834 North 41st Avenue, Glendale, Arizona 85308
www.winmarkcom.com
Phone: (602) 789-9240 • kaswinmark@yahoo.com

The Legend of Dynamite George -- The Poem
used with permission by Patrick G. Metoyer
Copyright © 2010 by Patrick G. Metoyer.   All rights reserved
Email contact: metoyer.poetry@gmail.com

Designed by David R Dawson
drdawson1@gmail.com

Library of Congress Cataloging-in-Publication Data
Registration Number TXu 1-680-293
Bennett, Carroll
The Legend of Dynamite George
Includes original photographs, glossary, and graphics

ISBN 978-1-892225-21-4

Printed in the United States of America

Acknowledgments

Without the encouragement and assistance of my family and friends, The Legend of Dynamite George would not have been published.

My mother, Betty Bennett, inspired me to write this story. When I was suffering from breast cancer, she was a constant source of encouragement. She would display my pack rat photos to distract me from my sickness. She knew my experiences with uranium miners in the Rocky Mountain States would form the basis for an entertaining book with Dynamite George as the central character. Her insistence that I complete the story and publish it proved to be the motivation I needed to focus on wellness rather than my illness.

I especially want to thank Margaret Kahn Garaway for encouraging me to work on this book in the 1980's when I lived with her and her husband, Marty, on the Navajo Reservation where I taught photography and recovered from cancer.

A dear friend, Joan Davidson of Tucson, has earned my thanks for meticulously editing my manuscript three times. Jennifer Frandsen dutifully typed and transcribed those early manuscripts.

So many of my friends supported me through this process. Jenny and Dave Dawson opened their home on Saturday afternoons while we worked on reading and changing the text of the book. Dave, an excellent graphic artist, did the line drawings in the front of the book. He also designed the book and helped me choose the photos and illustrations. Kas Winters of Winmark Communications Family Books and Resources, www.winmarkcom.com, provided extensive knowledge of printing and publishing. Her moral support is deeply appreciated.

Two doctors supported and encouraged me in this endeavor: Dr. Robert Sammons, M.D., Ph.D., and his staff; Joel Bechtel, M.D., who continued the care and treatment of Geno Saccomanno's, M.D., Ph.D., uranium miner lung-cancer patients.

I also want to thank all of the miners I met on my journey to the underworld. Dee Haight, a Wyoming miner, had a pet named "George"—whose nest was in an explosives magazine at the mine! Without this real-life pack rat, my story may never have emerged from the depths of my imagination.

Patrick G. Metoyer contributed to the final editing and wrote the introductory poem.

Map of The
Legend of
Dynamite George

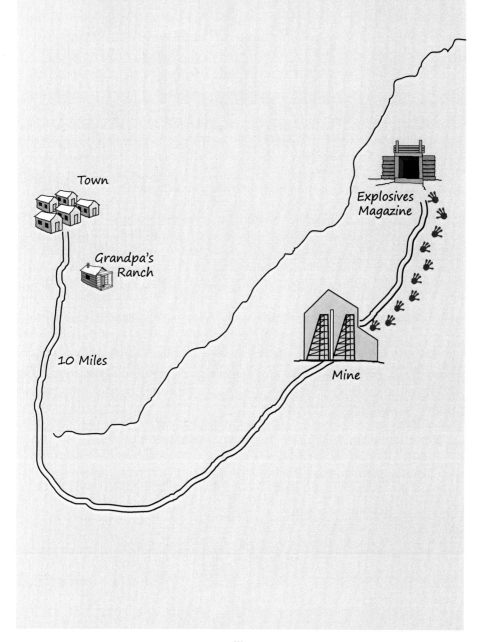

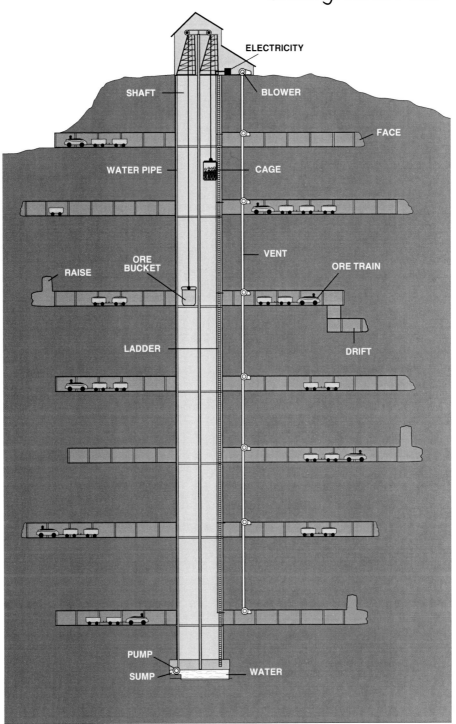

Underground Mine

ELECTRICITY

SHAFT

BLOWER

FACE

WATER PIPE

CAGE

VENT

RAISE

ORE BUCKET

ORE TRAIN

LADDER

DRIFT

PUMP

SUMP

WATER

Dedicated to the American workers and farmers,
both men and women, who endure hardships
to make our country great.

Another publication by Carroll Bennett:

Kikko's Tracks

Author's Notes

I graduated from Northern Arizona University in 1974 then worked at the Museum of Northern Arizona as a photographer. The museum received a National Park Service grant to do an ecological survey of the Grand Canyon to learn how the Glen Canyon Dam changed the Colorado River. I matched many of John Wesley Powell's Grand Canyon photographs to show the changes that had taken place in the previous one hundred years. When the survey was completed, I accepted a new employment offer in Grand Junction, Colorado.

I became a field technician for Dr. Geno Saccomanno, M.D., Ph.D., a pathologist working at St. Mary's Hospital on an epidemic of lung cancer in uranium miners. From our base in Grand Junction, we technicians drove a medical trailer from one mine site to the next in four Rocky Mountain states to collect sputum samples, which were later analyzed by hospital cytologists and pathologists.

This health-field experience of working with miners gave me insight into their world. Many of our health tests had to be done underground where the miners were in jeopardy of contracting lung cancer if they did not wear their masks or have the proper ventilation to keep down the dust.

In the Great Basin of Wyoming, I met a mine demolition expert, Dee Haight. His pet pack rat "George" lived in a nest in the mine's explosives magazine. Federal regulations prohibited flammable materials in proximity of the explosives. When George and his nest were evicted, the miners were angry.

Their concern for George—and all pack rats—is reflected in the numerous pack rat tales and legends in the west. One traditional folktale holds that when a pack rat senses trouble, it runs out of the mine; and the miners follow close behind. My story adds to the lore and is a testament to the "let live" attitude miners have for pack rats. George, of course, became Dynamite George—the central character in my account of a fictional mining world.

Pack rat and underground photos in my story are my original images. They were taken when I conducted lung-cancer tests underground during the late 1970's before cell phones, the Internet, and computers in schools and homes. The images do not represent today's mining technology.

Episodes involving the Mine Safety and Health Administration (MSHA) are purely fictional. Below is a brief explanation of the federal law authorizing the United States Department of Labor to protect miners in hard rock and coal mines:

> The Mine Safety and Health Administration administers provisions of the Federal Mine Safety and Health Act of 1977 and enforces mandatory safety and health standards to eliminate fatal accidents, to reduce the frequency and severity of nonfatal accidents, to minimize health hazards, and to promote improved safety and health conditions in the mining industry. *Public Law 91-173*

After my lung-cancer research project, I worked for MHSA and Colorado State University. Now retired, I work with digital imaging, photography, and writing.

Carroll Bennett – Spring 2010
Grand Junction, Colorado

NOTE: Lung cancer among uranium miners is mentioned in the book. Prior to my work at St. Mary's Hospital, Dr. Geno Saccomanno testified with other pathologists at Hearings of the Joint Committee on Atomic Energy, 91st Congress, January 28, 1970, on lung cancer research of uranium miners. His dedication in helping to change mining laws to protect uranium miners resulted in many lives being saved. These laws were included in the Federal Mine Safety and Health Act of 1977.

The Legend of Dynamite George

The Mining Pack Rat

Carroll Bennett

Table of Contents

The Legend of Dynamite George

The Poem

This is a tale of a frisky young pack rat
Dynamite George was his name
He roamed o'er the desert in search of adventure
This tale is a tale of his fame

He's known for his antics and playfulness too
His story is told far and wide
Come learn of this story – why he's cherished by all
Is his story for real – only you can decide

PROLOGUE

WHOOSH!

Claws shut like steel traps, catching a few hairs of the pack rat's bushy tail as it disappeared through a crack underneath a rusty iron door.

The great horned owl's body vibrated as it slammed against the massive door. Stunned and missing its prey, the owl staggered backwards, trying to balance on its taloned feet. Shaking its feathers into place, it blinked its large yellow-rimmed black eyes and searched the crack for the pack rat.

The owl spread its powerful wings then unsteadily lifted off the ground into the quiet night. It resumed its slow flight pattern, circling Sheep Mountain in search of a slower rodent.

The shivering pack rat climbed up on an oak beam behind the massive door. His radar ears listened for the owl's movements.

Sensing danger, his pink buttoned nose and long, quivering black whiskers worked in a frenzy. His protruding black eyes peered into the dark cavern which had been carved into the mountainside.

The pack rat crept along the rough beam above the door. He listened for the rustle of the owl's wings. The only sounds outside were the soft night breezes stirring the juniper and piñon trees.

The small animal's mountain cavern refuge was filled with a strange acrid smell.

He was out of danger for the first time since leaving his mother's nest. For weeks he had been chased by coyotes, ferrets and badgers, and tonight, by the greatest terror of all, a great horned owl with its extended talons swooping silently down from the black sky.

He stopped shivering as the fear of the owl's attack began to subside. He held his tail in his paws and licked the damaged fur with his tongue. Satisfied with his grooming, the exhausted pack rat wrapped his undernourished body with his warm bushy tail, curled into a ball, and slept.

A desert wind blew up the mountainside and rattled the signs that had been posted above the iron door and nailed to the surrounding trees.

DANGER! EXPLOSIVES! NO SMOKING! NO TRESPASSING! KEEP OUT!

But the small pack rat slept on, blissfully unaware of the warnings.

Chapter I
POWDER MONKEY DREAMS

Jamie Claybourne stuck his head out the window of the battered, faded blue 1963 Chevy pickup truck, Clarabelle, trying to control his anger. A dust devil from the desert floor encircled the old vehicle, giving it a good shaking, before whirling on up the mountain road. Coughing from the dust, Jamie ducked his head back into the cab and tried to roll up the rattling window.

He was hot, but not from the summer sun. "We'll never get enough money to get rid of this heap and buy a new truck if you ground me again from working as a mining intern, Grandpa," he grumbled.

"You're lucky I didn't ground you for the rest of the year," his grandfather, Lee Claybourne, answered, his light gray eyes flashing in anger.

"I still can't believe you would do something so stupid. Good thing I found those blasting caps sticking out of your backpack. You could have blown off your fingers or a hand fooling around with them."

Jamie thought his Grandpa Lee, as Jamie sometimes called him, did not understand that he just wanted to experiment with the detonator caps.

Two weeks earlier Jamie had received his internship to help his grandfather run errands at the mine. He received permission from the mine superintendent, Harry Groves, to go with his grandfather and the mine foreman, Mick Kelly, to see how explosives were used in the mine.

What an experience, Jamie thought. First the miners drilled a series of holes into the rock face that was to be blasted away. Then they opened boxes of the explosive ammonian nitrate, called Prell, which looked like small round pellets of snow. Three-Fingers Ralph Hall dumped a box of pellets into what looked like an upright vacuum cleaner and a hose blew the explosive particles into each drill hole until it was packed tight.

After thirty holes were filled, the miners asked his grandfather to take Jamie back to a safer place. He wanted to stay, but Mick gave him a stern look and he quickly obeyed.

From a safe distance he watched as the miners connected the fuses to the safety caps and placed them in the drill holes, crimping the fuses together and connecting them with a long leader fuse. The men then lit the long fuse to blow the rock face. The fuse started to burn with a sputtering red glow, giving all of them time to return to the electric train and leave the area before the explosion.

After seeing how the explosive caps worked like fire crackers, Jamie plotted to sneak a few from his grandfather's explosives building and set them off under tin cans. His plan was foiled, however, when his grandfather saw the orange fuses sticking out the top of Jamie's backpack. Jamie was still smarting from the tongue-lashing his grandfather had given him and the unfairness of being grounded for so long, just for being curious.

It was six o'clock Monday morning, and the July sun was already scorching Jamie's skin at the high elevation as he and his grandfather made their way slowly up the steep mountain road to the mine. Jamie squinted his eyes from underneath his yellow DuPont Explosives cap. He stared indignantly out at the vast Red Desert below. The sound of the ancient truck's tires on the rough surface seemed to be singing to Jamie about the vein of ore: Blast the ore! Blast the ore! Blow the vein! Blow the vein!

His grandfather down shifted his beloved pickup. He spun the tires on the loose gravel while trying to keep his eyes on the ledge of a narrow horseshoe curve.

"Be careful, Grandpa!" Jamie yelped.

Grandpa Lee, trying to suppress a smile at his backseat driver, tightened his lips, making his salt and pepper whiskers stand out. His smug expression just about drove Jamie crazy.

"You weren't fair about those blasting caps," protested Jamie. "I asked you to show me how to set off a few caps and you wouldn't listen to me!"

His intense blue eyes glared stubbornly at his grandfather from his dusty freckled face as he shoved his unruly, coppery red hair back under the yellow cap. He guessed he had about as much chance as a dog gnawing through rock of persuading his Grandpa Lee to let him have anything to do with explosives. All his grandfather and the mine officials would allow him to do was cut the harmless orange fuses and run errands.

"I've told you a hundred times, Jamie. Blasting caps are not toys, and setting off explosives in drill holes is dangerous, even for grown men! We thought you would get the message when you went underground and saw the force which explosives had on rock."

Thirteen-year-old Jamie had come to live with his grandfather after his father was killed in a mining cave-in several months before. Jamie was five years old when his mother, unhappy with life in a dusty mining town, left home. She filed for divorce and was never heard from again.

After his son's funeral, his grandfather brought Jamie back to Homestead, Wyoming with him. Moving his only grandson to Wyoming was the hardest thing his grandfather had ever done, as Jamie did not want to leave Arizona and all his friends. He had tried to talk to Jamie. For weeks the moody boy only responded with grunts of "yeh" and "no." His grandfather was relieved when Jamie started to show an interest in going up to the mine with him, asking questions about mining and what a demolitions expert did.

Harry Groves, the mine superintendent, understood Lee Claybourne's predicament when Jamie's dad was killed in a cave-in. He told Lee that Jamie could work at the mine in a summer intern program for teenagers. When Jamie became an intern, his grandfather was pleased to teach his grandson all he knew about mining; but he did not anticipate Jamie's eagerness to handle explosives. Now he wondered if he could trust Jamie after this episode with the blasting caps.

"Jamie, promise me you won't fool around with the caps again," pleaded his Grandpa Lee. "And to remind you of how dangerous they are did I tell you the story--"

Jamie muttered under his breath, not wanting to hear one of his grandfather's long-winded tales. Lee stopped talking and glanced over at Jamie's slouched form.

"What'd you say, Jamie?"

"Nothing."

"You're not even up to a donkey's ear yet and wanting to do a man's work," protested Grandpa Lee. "If any of them mining inspectors, especially Traitor Jack Campbell, knew you handled caps, I'd be fired in no time flat. Plus the mine would be fined. The Feds got regulations for everything."

Listening to his grandpa talk about his height made Jamie swell up like a horny toad. Not getting his way with setting the caps was bad enough, but mentioning his size was a sore point. Jamie, who was just over five feet tall, all legs and arms, only came up to his grandfather's chest. Lee was a big man, over six feet tall, like all of the Claybourne men.

Most of Jamie's friends in Arizona were taller than he was and he had to defend himself when they teased him about being a runt.

He had always wanted to grow up big like his dad and hear folks say, "Jamie, you're just like your dad," instead of, "Well, the boy sure didn't take after the Claybournes."

Stubbornly, Jamie stuck to the main issue, "But Grandpa, at the funeral you promised me when I moved to Wyoming with you, you'd teach me to be a demolitions man like you someday."

"Not to set off caps," answered his grandfather.

"Dad woulda been proud of me learning about explosives and how I work at the mine. They wouldn't let us near the big copper mine where dad worked."

"If your dad knew you snuck off with caps, he would have taken a belt to your hide," grumbled Grandpa, "and my hide too."

Jamie gritted his teeth and rubbed the dust from his itching nose. By the set of grandfather's whiskered jaw and the way his laugh wrinkles went into hiding around those steel-gray eyes, Jamie knew he was in serious trouble.

Grandpa Lee started to spin yarns about elf-like creatures called "Tommy Knockers" who haunted the mines and caused trouble. But then he started talking about losing his son, Johnny, in the mining accident.

"Jamie, your dad was my only child and he wasn't one to take chances when he mined. When I saw that coffin with my Johnny locked inside, dead from someone else's carelessness, it nearly killed me. Your dad was the best long-hole driller west of the Mississippi. Them day shifters, in their rush to get home, didn't follow safety rules and check the roof rock after they blasted."

Choking up, Grandpa Lee tried to squint back tears. "Yep. The geologists forgot to check after the blasting, too. Johnny just figured they'd checked out that weak rock, so he started to drill in that fault area."

"My Johnny could out-drill any miner, and I've see 'em fall to their knees trying to keep up with him," Grandpa Lee drifted off, looking out through the morning's haze.

Jamie blinked hard, reliving that night. He'd been listening to the CB scanner when sirens screamed from the mine. Turning up the volume he had heard the scanner crackle: "A cave-in, at 12 Level, and it got Claybourne. They're digging him out now."

Clarabelle hit a deep rut and jolted Jamie back to the present. Looking up the steep road to the mine, Jamie tried again to remember how he got to the copper mine that night. All he remembered was being at the mine entrance when they brought the stretcher out with a blanket covering his dad. All he could see were his dad's big hands dangling along the sides of the stretcher.

How many more times would his grandfather go over that awful accident?

Grandpa Lee drove Clarabelle through the open gates of the mine's chain link fence. He realized how upset Jamie was with the talk of the explosive caps and his father's death.

"All I wanted to do was learn about mining," Jamie said in a sad voice.

"Now, son, you'll learn mining and become the first Claybourne mining engineer. Mining is in your blood. Your great-great-granddaddy came from Cornwall to mine the West," said his grandfather, trying to lighten Jamie's spirit.

"But, Grandpa, you aren't listening to me. I know other boys in town are sneaking off with blasting caps and setting them off. They brag about being powder monkeys when they get out of vocational school. I just wanted you to set off a few caps with me so I would know what they were like. And you wouldn't," Jamie challenged.

"They're not getting blasting caps out of my stores," Grandpa Lee snorted angrily. "Wait and see. One of those smart alecks will blow off some fingers. That's the reason the caps are locked up."

"I thought if the kids knew I blew off a few caps they'd stop teasing me about riding in this old battered wreck you drive. I don't know why you didn't drive Dad's new pickup back up here.

You keep telling me it wasn't paid for but there was some insurance money too."

"How many times do I have to tell you I couldn't afford the payments on a new truck and the ranch? And your dad's insurance is for your education."

Clarabelle clattered to a stop in front of an aluminum building posted with explosives and danger signs.

"Grab the lunch buckets and thermos while I go unlock the door," Grandpa Lee said. "Stop being so mad at me for catching you. You need to make some new friends in town."

"Grandpa, I don't like shooting jackrabbits and chasing antelope and wild horses the way the boys in town do on their dirt bikes. Even if I did, I wouldn't be a part of that gang," Jamie answered. "They think I'm different and I don't fit in."

Jamie's voice trailed off. He thought of his friends in Arizona. "My best friend George and I didn't get off on stuff like that. I wish he were here with me. Why did Dad have to die?"

Lee was silent and the tension faded between them. There were no words for the pain they shared. Before he got out of the truck, he reached over with a long arm and squeezed Jamie's slight shoulders to give him reassurance. Jamie choked up thinking about his dad and slid closer to his grandfather, comforted by the familiar smells of cedar smoke, the morning's sausages and the acrid odor of explosives in his grandpa's denim coveralls.

The small, undernourished pack rat was busily arranging sticks and placing cedar boughs on the framework of his nest. For three nights he had worked from sunset until the early morning sun streaked through the bottom crack of the storage chamber door. This morning the nest was ready. The pack rat poked two Canadian Jay feathers and a candy wrapper into the center of the nest and crawled in. Smelling chocolate from the candy wrapper, he curled up into a ball and fell into an exhausted sleep, unaware of all the activity taking place a mile down the mountain at the mine.

Chapter II
DYNAMITE GEORGE TAKES OVER

Grandpa Lee and Jamie arrived at the large aluminum building which housed the mining office. The day shift miners stood around drinking coffee and joking about the donkey baseball team coming to Homestead for the company's Fourth of July barbecue picnic.

"Hey, Jamie, are ya gonna be the batboy for the donkeys?" Mick Kelly called out.

"Donkeys?" Jamie questioned.

Tall and gruff, Mick said, "We're counting on you to get them animals around the bases, Jamie." With a sparkling green eye he winked at Lee. Jamie's face reddened from Mick's teasing.

As soon as the day shifters were told where they would be working, they headed for the change room to put on their boots and waterproof diggers. The miners told Jamie to be careful of the Tommy Knockers when he was underground. "They're making lots of strange sounds and causing problems on Level Seven," one miner said.

Jamie shivered. The old mining superstition filled him with a spooky feeling as he followed his grandfather toward the explosives building.

"Grandpa, wait," Jamie called out, trying to catch up with his grandfather's long strides, the lunch buckets banging against his legs as he ran.

Entering the explosives building, Jamie shoved the black lunch buckets onto the counter alongside the ropes of orange fuses. He opened his locker and took out his boots and mining hat.

"Look at that grasshopper," Mick boomed as he came through the door. "Jamie, you're all legs and feet."

Jamie blushed. Onto his mining belt, he hooked a self-contained self-rescuer and the battery that was attached to the cap lamp. He hooked the lamp onto his hardhat and tested the light.

Mick looked out the door of the explosives building and saw the miners standing around the change room in their diggers instead of heading for the mineshaft.

"Hey guys, quit goofing off and get underground. It's gonna be noon already and you're not gonna get a bonus check by hangin' around and chewing the fat," Mick scolded.

Mick surveyed the fuses and detonator caps before turning to Lee.

"Lee, you and Jamie go on up the mountain to the explosives magazine. We're running low at all the stations and we gotta shoot off a lot of rounds today if we're ever gonna find some good ore and meet our quota."

"Great, I get to go up the mountain where the explosives are stored," Jamie said with anticipation.

Jamie thought how boring most days were as he sat in the explosives building measuring out the long orange fuses. The fuses were used with the blasting caps. He would have preferred being with his grandfather while he delivered explosives and caps to the miners underground. The explosives were stored on all levels of the mine in dry wooden storage bins called powder magazines.

Grandpa Lee and Jamie left the small white building with Mick and headed for the mining company's white 4X4 truck. Jamie was impressed with the bright red lettering on the truck doors warning: EXPLOSIVES.

Lee and Mick watched the boy climb into the truck. "I know just how the boy feels," Mick said. "I was fourteen when my dad died in a mine explosion. I was the oldest and had to go to work in the mines to feed my ma, kid sisters and brothers. In those days there were no safety regulations."

Lee nodded in agreement. He watched his grandson sitting alone in the truck and thought the boy should be in town playing with kids his own age.

"At times Jamie thinks the whole world is against him. When the other boys get friendly and tease him about Clarabelle, he thinks they're insulting him."

Mick, with his eyes on Jamie, rubbed his chin. "It'll take him a while to get used to Wyoming. I've seen a change in the boy since you've been teaching him about mining."

"Yeh, I know. He got it in his head he only wants to know about explosives. But gradually he is picking up a lot about mining. He wants to be a powder monkey. If he could just find something he was interested in besides the mine. It ain't natural for him not making new friends," Lee added.

"Just hope the feds don't find him working in explosives, Lee," Mick warned. "Running errands for the office, and cutting fuses is enough for this summer."

"You're right, Mick. Them feds would be down on us like angry bees," Lee answered.

"Maybe when school starts up next month he'll find some new friends and get into sports," Mick tried to reassure Lee. "My oldest gal, Fran, just finished college and she'll be coming home soon. She'll be teaching junior high. If Jamie's in her class, I'll guarantee she'll get him interested in something."

"Sure hope so," Lee said quietly. "He spent Sunday alone out in the desert again. He mopes around like he's in a daze and if he's not careful, he's going to stumble over a rattler."

"Give him time, Lee," Mick said, "things will work out all right."

Impatiently, Jamie watched Mick and his grandfather talking in the road. Mick reminded him of his dad, full of fun and devilish humor. He admired his grandfather, who was serious about his work and still mining when he could be retired. He had been mining for forty years, except for a stint in the Second World War, and he was still a hard-working miner. With a glint in his eyes, Jamie slid into the driver's seat and started the engine of the truck. His grandfather's head jerked up. His face reddened and he took off in huge bounding strides for the truck. Mick stood laughing in the road.

"Why, you banty rooster," snorted Grandpa Lee, "Get out from behind that wheel."

"That got your attention. Let's go," Jamie said with a laugh and slid from behind the wheel.

His grandfather shifted the truck into gear and shot forward. Startled, Jamie looked at his grandpa's whiskered face and saw those familiar smile-crinkles around his light gray eyes. He laughed at his grandpa, four-wheeling the company truck up the mountain road to the explosives magazine.

A mile up the steep road they came to a dead end. Lee stopped the truck at the front entrance of the wooden explosives magazine, located inside of Sheep Mountain.

Stern warnings in red marked the area around the magazine. Signs were posted on the large iron door, nailed onto trees, and bolted to rocks. DANGER! EXPLOSIVES! NO TRESPASSING! UNAUTHORIZED PERSONNEL KEEP OUT! The message was clear.

A massive, rusty iron door opened into a small room. Inside, a second iron door, lined with oak, opened into a large cavern where the explosives were stored. Heavy padlocks secured both doors to keep out thieves and trespassers.

The door into the cavern was made of wood so nothing could create a spark to set off the explosives stored in fifty pound crates away from the doors. Prell (ammonian nitrate) an explosive, could easily ignite from too much heat or friction and blow off the top of the mountain. For added safety, the explosive caps and fuses were locked in the explosives building a mile below at the mine, far from the Prell.

Jamie felt uneasy watching his grandpa fumble in his baggy pinstriped overalls for the key chain. It was always so quiet and eerie up here, and knowing what was stored inside the mountain side made it even creepier. He remembered his grandpa's stories of how he received a medal in World War II for sneaking up behind enemy lines and blowing up their demolition stores.

Grandpa Lee unlocked the padlock and shoved the massive iron door open. A skittering and rustling sound came from the small dark room. Jamie and his grandfather jerked backward in surprise. At first Jamie thought it might be a rattlesnake slithering across the floor toward them. Quickly he turned on the bright miner's lamp on his hardhat and, in the circle of the searchlight beam, he saw a small creature, about the size of a prairie dog, or a squirrel, or a . . . ?

While trying to keep the light beam on the scurrying creature, Jamie stumbled over a pile of twigs and rubbish piled right in the middle of the floor.

"What is it, Grandpa? Look, it's trying to build a nest in here!" Jamie yelled, chasing the tawny creature's movements with his light beam. When the small animal was finally cornered, it jumped up to a log beam and froze in the light.

The critter was like nothing Jamie had ever seen before. Its ears were a translucent pink, and stuck out like radar antennas from a pointed face. Its bulbous pink nose wiggled in a frenzy, and long black whiskers quivered and fanned the air. Its glittering black eyes watched Jamie's every move while its small pink hind feet drummed out a warning. Jamie laughed quietly at this small brazen creature threatening him.

"Grandpa, it's a rat with a long bushy tail! And did you see him take off?"

"Well, I'll be danged. That's a half-growed male pack rat. He's got some nerve. He's got no more business in an explosives magazine than a skunk has in a lady's bedroom. If that critter started gnawing on the explosives, he'd get us blowed sky high."

"Look at all the junk he's brought in here," Jamie said, studying the cornered pack rat and the mess on the floor.

"Yep, he's moving in. And this is probably just the beginning of his mess."

The pack rat looked down at the intruders and continued stamping his hind feet and chattering his teeth angrily.

"Do you think there are any more?"

"No, son. They're loners."

"Like me?" Jamie sighed, still studying the pack rat. "Do you think I can make friends with him?"

"I believe you can, Jamie, since he's only half-growed. When I was a boy, I tamed a few young'uns like him by feeding them peanuts," Grandpa Lee reminisced. "I got them so tamed they ate out of my pockets."

"I know I can tame him and make him like me."

Grandpa Lee studied Jamie's eager face and didn't have the heart to tell him that the pack rat and his nest were against government mining regulations.

His grandfather sighed in resignation, "O.K., he can stay. But the first time he gets through that second door into the explosives, he has to go. Pack rats are nothing but trouble."

"We'll keep him a secret, Grandpa."

"Mick has to know. He'll understand because at one time pack rats were thought to be good luck to miners."

"How come, Grandpa?"

"Mines weren't so big and deep in the old days and the pack rats lived inside the tunnels. The miners felt safe having them nearby because a pack rat can hear weak rock, timbers giving, and underground water long before a human can. When a pack rat lit out from a mine, a miner was right behind that bushy tail."

"I wish a pack rat had been in the mine with Dad to warn him of that weak roof that killed him."

"Same here. But pack rats are nothing but a nuisance nowadays. With all this new-fangled mining equipment they can make a lot of trouble."

"What kind of trouble?"

"They're always packing off something to their nests that the miners need. One reason they're called pack rats and trade rats is 'cause they carry off shiny things. On the way to their nests, if they see something else, they drop what they have and trade it. They're funny critters 'til they pack off somethin' of yours you value."

"Grandpa, he won't get into trouble up here."

"Don't count on it, Jamie. He's busy building his nest right now. It won't be long before he finds the mine and starts packing off things."

"What happens if he bothers the miners' things?"

"They usually trap 'em and put 'em back in the desert where they belong."

"They don't hurt them?"

"Depends. Pack rats can cause a lot of trouble."

"Look, he's acting sleepy."

"He's nocturnal - a night animal. He gathers his food and builds his nest at night. Only swing shift and grave yard shift have to worry about him," answered his grandfather. He opened the inner door and entered the large wood-lined cavern to get the crates of explosives to take to the mine.

"Jamie, hold the door open and make sure the pack rat doesn't get in here," warned Grandpa Lee. Jamie stood to the side of the door, blocking the pack rat's access to the explosives room. "You stay outta here," threatened Jamie when he noticed the pack rat's glittering black eyes focus on the opening to the dark cavern.

Grandpa Lee hefted a crate of explosives onto his shoulder and carefully loaded them onto the truck. Jamie, in the meantime, guarded the door. As he kept his eye on the tawny creature, he thought about what to call him.

Maybe, Bushy Tail, he thought. Or Radar, because of his big ears? How about Fleet, for how fast he moved? Why not a human name for a special friend?

"Grandpa, is it okay to use a human name for him?"

"Sure. But I hope you don't plan to name him after your dad."

"No. I'm gonna name him for my best friend in Arizona, George."

Jamie followed his grandfather out of the explosives magazine and watched the large door shut. "Grandpa, I'm gonna name him Dynamite George, instead of just George, because he lives in the explosives magazine." A smile crossed Jamie's lips and he felt very pleased with the new name.

That night, Jamie woke from a dream. He had been dreaming that the perky pack rat was riding on his shoulder while he explored the tunnels and drifts of the mine. In the dream, Jamie was setting off explosions and blasting away tons of ore to earn a large Christmas bonus check.

Rubbing his eyes, Jamie slipped out of bed and went to the window. He looked out at the dark shadow of the mountain and at the mining tower light, blinking brightly, showing the mine's location.

What was Dynamite George doing? Jamie wondered as he stared at the light. The desert breeze was cool in July, and usually comforting, but Jamie felt a chill. He went back to his warm bed and his dreams.

Dynamite George sat on the large beam until the only sound he could hear was the cool desert breeze blowing up the mountain. He then gathered the scattered sticks, twigs and pieces of candy wrapper Jamie had stumbled over. Carefully he rebuilt his nest in a safer spot in the corner of the small room. When he finished, he curled into a ball, wrapped his bushy tail around himself and went to sleep.

The following evening Dynamite George left the explosive magazine again to search for new material for his nest. He found small green juniper branches, larkspur, pieces of bark, and delicious-smelling candy wrappers blown up the mountain from the mine site. Occasionally, he would stop to bite the tops off wild flowers. He nibbled at the lichen growing on the rocks, greedily gobbling them down and then licking the salt and minerals from his whiskers.

The explosive magazine was a perfect place for his nest. It was safer than living under a rock ledge. It was an excellent place to store his winter food, as the area held a bountiful supply of nuts, berries, dried grasses, mushrooms and lichen.

On the fourth night of gathering food and material for his nest, he noticed the blinking light below. This night he heard many different sounds in the distance and smelled fumes in the air. He abandoned his search for nesting material and curiously followed the small game trails down the mountain toward the sounds.

As he neared the mine site, the rumble from the air compressors, which forced fresh air underground to the miners, thundered in his sensitive ears. Wincing from the noise, he ran underneath an upright steel tower. Above him, a steel frame supported cables that carried ore buckets from underground. The ore buckets were emptied into waiting trucks to be taken to the mill.

Flying projectiles scattered near Dynamite George, and he found shelter under a front-end loader. Crouching beneath a large rubber tire, he felt safe from all the noise and confusion. He watched the whole scene from that spot, following the lumbering movements of the heavy equipment going back and forth. Suddenly his shelter roared and rattled around him, filling the air with diesel fumes as the engine started. The tire jerked forward and he leapt, just in time, through the entrance door of a large building.

The night shift mechanics and welders were doing some repairs on a piece of mining machinery, and an acrid smell lingered after each flash of flame from the welding equipment.

To escape the brilliance of the welding flames, Dynamite George leapt to the wall. It was covered with foam siding and provided good footing for his sharp toenails. He scampered up the wall to a large steel support beam where he crouched, surveying the scene below. Squinting between flashes of the arc welding equipment, his eyes adjusted to the machine shop. So many things! So many bright shiny objects! Such a wealth of treasures!

The welders turned off their equipment at midnight and went to the lunchroom for their dinner break. Dynamite George boldly crept along the steel beam to the other end of the shop to investigate the place where the men had been working. He hopped down to the concrete floor, scampered over work benches, sniffed at the welding equipment, moved tools, tugged at welding masks, and ran underneath the large equipment. There he found his prize.

A large, crumpled leather work glove would be a part of his nest. He clutched the glove by the thumb with his four needle-sharp front teeth and dragged it across the shop floor to the door. He disappeared into the dark, pulling and tugging the glove across the road.

It was a long, hard climb up the mountainside. The glove, snagging on sticks and catching between rocks, somersaulted him backwards. He worried and fought the glove up the mountain until at last he arrived at the explosives magazine. Clutching his prize, with a last great effort he pulled the glove into the safety of his nest and collapsed into its center, worn to a frazzle.

Chapter III
FOURTH OF JULY

Every morning since the discovery of Dynamite George, Jamie jumped from bed, ate breakfast and helped pack the lunch buckets. He'd quit harassing his grandfather about Clarabelle's laboring progress uphill to the mine and had stopped nagging about setting charges and blasting for ore. He was consumed with his plans to tame Dynamite George.

At first Jamie left small piles of peanuts on the wooden floor by the entrance to the nest. When the sleepy pack rat poked his head out of his nest to investigate the smells, Jamie would keep still and softly talk to him.

The piles of peanuts were hoarded away after Jamie left. Soon Dynamite George began to associate peanuts with Jamie's soft voice. When the peanuts were passed under his nose and long twitching whiskers, he would grab them from Jamie's fingers. Dynamite George became so greedy for peanuts he would sleep, listening with his radar ears, for the sound of the laboring engine of the truck as it wound its way up the mountain. When the massive door swung open, he was already out of his nest, standing on his back feet and sniffing the air for his handout.

"Grandpa, he's learning to trust me," Jamie said, as Dynamite George grabbed peanut after peanut with his pink paws, packing each one safely away in his nest.

Slowly, Jamie reached out to stroke the silky russet coat. Alarmed, Dynamite George dashed up the wall to the safety of the oak beam.

Jamie left a pile of peanuts in front of the nest.

"Grandpa, he'll never let me touch him," Jamie said in exasperation.

"It takes patience to tame them wild critters," Grandpa Lee reassured Jamie. "You got him hooked on the peanuts and it won't be long before he'll be looking in your pockets for a handout."

Over the Fourth of July weekend, Jamie didn't have a chance to go up the mountain to leave peanuts for Dynamite George. Instead, he and Grandpa attended the barbecue celebration in Homestead. There he watched the men turn skewered beef over pits of hot coals, using large paintbrushes to coat the meat with red barbecue sauce. The whole town smelled deliciously of smoky roasting barbecue and ears of sweet corn bubbling in large iron cauldrons.

Children ran in and out of a large open air tent where tables were covered with cakes, cookies, salads, homemade pies and pickles. At one end of the tent, a group of men took turns churning ice cream.

Jamie felt a twinge of sadness when he heard the boisterous laughter from the men gathered around kegs of beer. His dad had always been in the center of such gatherings and told the best jokes and stories.

Between sumptuous platefuls of food, he watched the miners in a drilling contest. Straining bodies leaned against jackhammers as bits bored holes in sandstone slabs. Dad would have out-drilled all of them with one hand tied behind his back, Jamie thought to himself.

Lee Claybourne and Mick were sitting at a table with a group of sour-faced miners. The local union representative was explaining something about a forced investigation to find the source of all the ground water in Level Seven.

"I've mined in water over my boots before," one miner interrupted. "That's our richest vein of ore. You start an investigation and we won't see our Christmas bonus."

"Jest keep your mouth shut and stop stirring up trouble," one of the miners said bitterly to the union man. "We gotta mine in any conditions to make a living." Tempers flared as the union man told the miners they were crazy not to join a union and protect themselves.

Tired of the bickering and politics, and with three hours to kill before the donkey baseball game started, Jamie decided to cool off in the Sweetwater River north of town.

As he approached the swimming hole he heard catcalls and whistles from a group of rowdy teenagers swimming in the nude.

"Jump on in, rat-lover!" they jeered.

Red faced, Jamie turned away, feeling miserable and wondering how they heard about the pack rat. Slowly he wandered along the river to a quiet place among the rushes. He stripped down to his jockey shorts and immersed his body in the cool water, listening to the quiet gurgling of the river and the splashing and shouting teenagers downstream. Feeling drowsy, he returned to the riverbank and dozed until the harsh desert light softened and a breeze stirred him awake.

Jamie jumped up, awakened by the silence, and pulled on his Levis. He pushed through the rushes and hiked back on the dirt road to the picnic. He wanted to get to the bleachers to find a good seat before the donkey baseball game started. He sat down and waited for his grandfather, but he didn't come. He left the bleachers and found him sitting under the tent, talking to Mick about how it was in the old days when his ancestors worked in mines just using picks and shovels.

"Where ya been, Grasshopper?" Mick asked.

"Got tired and went down to the Sweetwater and cooled off in the river," Jamie answered. "Are you going to the donkey baseball game with me, Grandpa?"

"After I finish telling about the dinosaur I found in a mine in Trach," his grandfather answered.

Jamie knew when he heard the words Trachyte Canyon that his grandfather was telling one of his long-winded accounts of a dinosaur find. He waited impatiently until the end, and then they left for the bleachers.

The players were dressed up like clowns. The first batter hit the ball and mounted a small donkey, kicking it in the ribs to get to first base. The angry animal flattened its ears and bucked. The clown fell over its head with the reins still firmly gripped in his hand. When he got up and tried to remount, the donkey reached around with his long yellow teeth and chomped down on the clown's backside. The player let out a yell that could be heard all the way up the mountain. The crowd went wild with laughter and Jamie laughed so hard he could barely breathe.

The Fourth of July evening ended with a crescendo of fireworks, fire engine sirens, and, off in the distance at the mine, fireworks displaying the letter "H" for Homestead.

It had been a big day. Jamie climbed wearily into Clarabelle and was soon sound asleep. Lee let his exhausted grandson sleep as he drove to the ranch, glancing at him from time to time.

The Fourth of July fireworks and explosions frightened Dynamite George. He quivered with each loud boom, startled as the sky turned red and orange with each burst. He returned to the safety of his nest, too nervous to gather food or pick up any shiny objects. The explosions soon stopped and he curled into a ball and fell asleep.

On the steep uphill drive to the explosives magazine in the broiling July sun, Jamie told about the kids teasing him about being a rat lover. "How did they find out about Dynamite George?" Jamie asked.

"Nothing's a secret in a small place like Homestead. News travels fast and I suspect Mick told some of his young'uns."

"It was our secret, Grandpa!"

"Jamie, things have been disappearing from the mine and the men were fighting mad. They were blaming each other, so I told Mick. Remember son, this mine's got a big mixture of people from all over the country and many of them are tramp miners, going from mine to mine."

"Mick didn't warn me about having to get rid of Dynamite George," responded Jamie.

"You don't have to worry about Mick. It's the Federal Mining Inspectors you have to worry about. They got books full of rules and regulations they have to follow."

"Grandpa, do you think any of the miners will squeal on Dynamite George if we return all the stuff he carries up to the explosive magazine from the mine?" Jamie asked.

"I just hope that critter doesn't steal the wrong things. Then word will leak out about his nest and the Feds will be down on us as fast as a duck on a June bug," answered Grandpa Lee.

"If Johnny's old friend Traitor Jack hears about a pack rat nest near the explosives, he'll have to check on it. He hasn't checked the explosives magazine in years 'cause he knows I follow all government mining regulations."

"That's a funny name. Why Traitor Jack?" asked Jamie.

"Cause he took a job with the government, and some of the miners think it's a betrayal. When he was younger he could mine nearly as good as your dad but he got tired of seeing accidents and thought he could do more good as an inspector," answered his grandfather.

The truck stopped in front of the explosives magazine and Jamie jumped out, anxious to see Dynamite George.

A crack of light filtered through the large door and Jamie saw the young pack rat outside of his nest, his pink button nose sniffing for peanuts.

Jamie smiled and quietly approached, crushing the peanuts in his Levi pockets until an aroma of peanuts filled the small room. Jamie sat on the floor and let the hungry pack rat investigate the pockets of his blue jeans.

Dynamite George dug into each pocket, stuffing his mouth full of peanuts.

Cautiously, Jamie stroked the silky fur. Dynamite George bristled for a second, then continued his digging. A great warm feeling came over Jamie. He had succeeded in making the pack rat trust him and he bubbled up with happiness.

Days passed quickly for Jamie. Soon Dynamite George would climb onto Jamie's shoulder and search for peanuts hidden under his hardhat. He tried to force Jamie's fingers open with his paws, pushing his moist nose into Jamie's clutched fist, until he was rewarded by finding a nut.

Chapter IV
A CURIOUS YOUNG GIRL

The explosives truck rounded the sharp turn and squeaked to a stop in front of the door in the side of the mountain.

Perched on a rock directly under two signs which clearly read KEEP OUT and DANGER, sat a slender girl, about Jamie's age, with a face as pale as moonlight.

Waving to them, she jumped off the rock, landing lightly on her feet. Her long straw-colored hair bounced lightly on her frail shoulders.

"Hey! What're you doing up here?" Lee scolded. "Can't you read this area is posted?"

The slight girl shrugged her shoulders.

"Whose young'un are you anyway?" sputtered his grandfather. "You just wait 'til I tell your parents about your trespassing on mining property."

Jamie snickered at his grandfather trying to pretend outrage at the young girl.

The girl faced them defensively, her long fingers tightening into fists. "It's a free country. I just came up to see the rat," she said with her large hazel eyes in defiance.

"Pack rat," Jamie corrected.

Lee Claybourne and Jamie didn't know what to make of this young wisp of a girl in their territory. Sensing this, she changed her tone, smiled shyly and introduced herself.

"I'm Windy Bassett. My pa is William A. Bassett and my ma is Melanie Anne Bassett. We're from the coalfields of Gary, West Virginia. And I got twin brothers, Ted and Ned, and one younger sister, Laura Lou. I'm in the middle," Windy's voice rattled off the information at a machine gun rate.

Jamie eyed her under his mining hat and puffed up his chest, answering her with an air of authority.

"I'm Jamie Claybourne. This is my grandpa, Lee Claybourne. We handle the explosives and that is dangerous work. Ain't that so, Grandpa?" Jamie replied.

"You're right at that, Jamie," Grandpa Lee said. His eyes twinkled as he watched the youngsters size each other up.

"My real name is Winifred, but Ma says I talk too much and ask too many questions, so she calls me a windbag. Windy, for short."

"Where'd you hear about Dynamite George?" Jamie asked with concern.

"The Kelly boys told me about a pet rat living on top of dynamite." Windy fell silent for a second to gather her thoughts, and then continued.

"I read about 'em in a nature book on animals of the Great Basin Desert. So I came up here hoping you would let me see it," Windy's voice was soft and her eyes looked hopeful as she spoke to Jamie and his grandfather.

Jamie squirmed under the girl's gaze. Grandpa Lee's eyes narrowed down to look more keenly at this slight girl.

"Does it bite?" Windy asked, hoping they would let her see the pack rat.

"No. He hasn't bit Grandpa or me," Jamie said, walking toward the large iron door. He looked over at the girl and thought about how skinny and tall she was. He mumbled over his shoulder to her, "If you want to see Dynamite George, you gotta promise not to tell anyone else."

"I promise to keep it a secret," answered Windy.

Windy was so excited to share the secret that a flush reddened her face. Jamie, seeing how pretty she was when she blushed, offered her some peanuts to feed Dynamite George. She wasn't too bad for a girl, he thought, even though she was an inch or so taller than he was. It might be nice to know someone that was always in trouble for talking too much and asking too many questions.

Lee unlocked the large iron door. Windy passionately chattered on about what she had read in the book about animals of the desert.

"I know that this kind of rat likes to pack treasures to its nest, like magpies and ravens do. The book said they are also called 'Trade Rats' 'cause sometimes they'll drop what they are carrying and trade it for something new. What kinda stuff has your rat brought back to its nest?"

"Pack rat!" corrected Jamie defensively. "The most exciting thing he brought home was a flint arrowhead the Indians used to hunt prairie chickens."

"You two better be quiet. Hearing a strange voice might frighten him and he'll hide in the rafters," Grandpa Lee warned.

The heavy door squeaked as Grandpa swung it open. Jamie whispered to Windy, "Be patient and don't make any fast moves, okay?"

"Don't worry, I'm patient. I gotta be 'cause there's six of us crowded into that small trailer, plus the coon hounds. The town kids tease us about being hillbillies, and worse, they mimic the way I talk," Windy whispered back. Jamie sensed how unwelcome she felt in this Wyoming country.

"SShhh!" warned Jamie as they went into the small dark room. He tiptoed to the two-foot high nest which took up an entire corner. He then knelt down by the nest's entrance.

Speaking softly, Jamie said, "Hi, Dynamite George, I brought a new friend to meet you. See? She won't hurt you. Here's a peanut."

At the sound of Jamie's familiar voice, Dynamite George poked his sleepy head out of the nest and sniffed ravenously. Windy stood spellbound behind Jamie. Dynamite George stiffened at the sight of the stranger, his whiskers whipping the air. He came out of his nest slowly, one paw poised in mid-air, ready to dash to safety.

Jamie patiently held a peanut in his hand until Dynamite George's gluttony overcame his fear. "Now you try," Jamie said, giving a peanut to Windy. "Just be very quiet and still. Dynamite George needs to figure out if he can trust you."

Dynamite George eyed the quiet girl cautiously and, at last, he accepted her offering of a peanut.

Grandpa Lee stood back watching the two youngsters kneeling on the wooden floor feeding a fat, greedy pack rat. He chuckled to himself and rubbed his whiskers, remembering the days when he was the same age and how the kids used to come see the wild critters he had tamed.

"He took it!" exclaimed Windy. "He actually took the peanut from my fingers. He's so pretty and looks so soft. His little feet are like little hands when he takes the peanut from my fingers. He's the biggest rat I've ever seen!" Windy whispered.

"Windy, please call Dynamite George a pack rat," Jamie insisted. "He's not one of those ugly, gray rats. Can't you tell how different his coat is and how bushy his tail is? Plus he's smart."

"Okay," Windy said in an apologetic tone. "You're right. He's not at all like those nasty gray rats that used to get into our corn crib and cabin in West Virginia."

Windy leaned closer to Dynamite George as she fed him another peanut. She peered closely at the busy wiggling pink nose. His front paws moved quickly when he took the peanuts and he sat on his haunches to eat. When he finished, his tiny front feet blurred as he groomed his whiskers and face.

"He's so shiny and clean," exclaimed Windy. "He looks like he shampoos his hair every day."

Jamie observed that while the bushy-tailed pack rat was personally clean, his nest and collection were a disaster. "Dynamite George is getting himself into big trouble lately," confided Jamie.

"What's he doing?" Windy replied, moving closer to find out the secret.

"He's getting into the miners' lunch buckets and his favorite food is their Twinkies. He can carry off a whole package of two Twinkies," Jamie whispered, with a devilish grin, thinking of Dynamite George running off with a package of sticky sweets. "He's also brought up nuts and bolts from the machine shop and Harry the Mole's welding glove. We take what we can find to the mechanics so they won't get mad. That's the reason we are trying to keep him a secret."

"Pa says rats are a big nuisance at the mine. Is that so, Jamie?" Windy asked, looking at Jamie and understanding his love of this small creature.

"Most of the miners don't get that mad about his stealing. I just hope he doesn't take anything valuable. Right now he's collecting hay for winter," Jamie said, pointing to the different stacks of dried grasses.

"Maybe someday he'll let me pet him," Windy said hopefully. "Oh, he just looks so soft and cuddly!"

Grandpa Lee, struggling to load the large boxes of explosives, told Jamie he wasn't earning his keep. Jamie told Windy he had to get to work and stop goofing off because his grandpa depended on him.

"While all those other guys are playing around in Homestead, I'm up here with Grandpa working like a man. This way I get to learn all about explosives," Jamie bragged as he squared his slim shoulders.

After the truck was loaded, Grandpa closed and locked the iron door. The last Windy saw of Dynamite George was a fuzzy tail disappearing inside the huge mound of twigs.

Full of peanuts, Dynamite George curled up deep inside his nest, wrapped his tail around his body and went back to sleep.

Windy gladly accepted Grandpa's offer of a ride down to the mine. Grandpa put the explosives truck in low gear and cautiously drove down the steep mountain road. Windy wondered aloud whether the next time she saw Dynamite George, he might let her pet him while he searched for peanuts in her pockets. She told Jamie she felt happy for the first time since her family had moved to Wyoming from West Virginia.

Windy told Jamie she didn't feel like returning to the crowded trailer where her twin brothers were always arguing.

"Hey Jamie, do you think your grandpa would let me come today when you deliver the explosives to the mine?" she whispered, nudging Jamie secretively. "I've been inside an old coal mine, just once, with my brothers. We snuck in, but then we got scared there might be methane gas, and ran out."

Surprised by the girl's request, Jamie studied Grandpa's whiskered face, wondering if it was possible. Taking a girl underground might cause trouble, he thought, remembering the superstitions about how women going into mines were thought to bring bad luck such as fires, cave-ins or explosions.

Lee noticed the serious expressions on the youngsters' faces and heard them whispering. "Okay, you kids. What are you plotting?" his grandfather asked jokingly. He noticed that Jamie was enthused about sharing his experiences with the young West Virginian and she seemed happy to have found a new friend.

"Mr. Claybourne, Pa says uranium mining is a lot different than coal mining. Can I go down in the mine with you and Jamie today?" she pleaded. "I heerd my Pa talk about long-holing. He said this mine pays by the number of feet a miner drills, and all he talks about is how much money he's gonna make."

"That's called gypo. It's extra pay for the number of feet of ore you drill," answered Grandpa Lee.

"Sometimes you sound funny, Windy," Jamie said. "You say 'heerd' instead of heard."

"West Virginians talk different than we do," Grandpa Lee said, scratching his whiskers and thinking about how to answer Windy's request.

"Reckon I don't know if Harry Groves, the mine superintendent, will let you go below. We only have one delivery on Level Five today, and that won't take long," Grandpa Lee answered.

Each fall the mine had tours for school children and their families. The company wanted to impress on the town that the children should not play around the topside of the mine.

He hoped to ease his grandson's pain over the loss of his father and to keep him busy until school started. But Grandpa Lee didn't know if Harry would allow Windy to go underground. Maybe with a parent's permission, it would be all right.

"First we'll go to the mine office to ask," Grandpa Lee said.

Jamie watched his grandfather's face and realized what a softie he was. He knew Windy was going underground with them if Harry gave his permission.

"Person never gets an idea of how a mine operates if they stay topside," said Grandpa Lee. "If you go under, be sure and duck out of the way when I tell you to."

"Oh, I will!" exclaimed Windy.

Lee wondered why Windy's parents didn't keep a closer watch on their daughter. "When did your people move west, Windy?" he asked.

"Pa came out first in the spring and then we came out after school was out in June. It was hard to leave my friends," she said in a tight voice. "At least the trailer is nicer than the cabin, even if it's smaller. When my twin brothers are home, there is little room to eat dinner because the place is so small. The worst part is I have to sleep in a tiny room with my younger sister."

"Wow! I thought it was bad moving to Wyoming to live in a log cabin with Grandpa, but we have plenty of room," Jamie responded.

"There ain't no peace and quiet at home," said Windy. "The twins are always arguin' and Pa's coon hounds are always underfoot," she paused, her hazel eyes darkening. "That's one of the reasons I hike around in the desert, so I can be alone. Out there I just hear the wind and I love to watch the wild animals, especially the antelope."

"I like animals, too," Jamie answered, "and I've been collecting mineral specimens in the desert and from the mine. I have Grandpa's old Army ammunition bag to carry them in and then I look up the specimens in my dad's geology and mining books," Jamie answered.

Windy continued, "Back home, when the food stamps ran out, we lived on cornbread, pinto beans, fatback and greens for a whole year. So did everyone else. All the coal mines shut down...everyone was poor...no medicine if you got sick...it was awful. That's when Pa decided to tramp and go out west from mine to mine."

"It must have been hard living like that," said Jamie. "Do you get homesick?"

"I'm homesick all the time for my friends. But it's better out here for the family. Pa's working full time, and Ned and Ted are working part time as laborers at the mine."

"I've never had a real family. My mother left when I was five," Jamie said, "and Dad brought me up until he was killed in a mine accident. Now it's just me and Grandpa."

"Oh, Jamie, I didn't know. I thought you were up here for summer vacation with your Grandpa," Windy said gently.

"It's all right. Grandpa and I are getting use to each other. He just drives a clunker of a truck he calls Clarabelle and I'm ashamed to be seen in that ancient piece of junk. He's got no pride," whispered Jamie.

"I know just what you mean. I didn't want to be seen with Pa because he dresses like a hillbilly and he needs false teeth. The last two years, since the coal mines shut down, I sometimes pretend I don't belong to my family. Now that money is coming in, all Pa talks about is getting new teeth. Ned and Ted are saving for a four-by-four long bed pick-up. Pa said if there's any money left over, he's going to buy us school clothes. Most of the time I just get hand-me-downs."

They dropped off the boxes of Prell at the mine shaft and then drove to the explosives building. Windy helped Jamie crank out orange fuses for the blasting caps while Grandpa Lee packed the caps in wooden crates marked DANGER. Jamie was pleased to show Windy how much he knew about explosives.

Lee loaded the caps and fuses into the truck as he listened to the youngsters' excited chatter in the building.

"Windy sure was right," muttered the old miner, smiling to himself. "She asks about as many questions as Jamie does."

After they left the explosives building, Jamie and Grandpa took Windy to the mining office so they could ask Harry if she could go underground with them. As they approached the secretary, Windy felt self-conscious, and her pale face turned pink when Grandpa introduced her as "Billy's young'un."

"Go on in," Lorraine said warmly. "Harry's on the phone to the Mine, Safety and Health Administration with his usual complaints about their inspections."

Windy could hear the angry man talking on the phone and had a sinking sensation he would never let her go with Jamie and Grandpa Lee. With a few select words, Harry finally hung up the phone. When he saw his three visitors, his face changed from a frown to a smile.

"What's up, Lee? And where did you and Jamie find this pretty girl?" he asked, winking at Windy.

"This is Windy Bassett!" Jamie answered.

"She's Billy's kid. He works graveyard," said Grandpa Lee, preparing for the big question. "Is it all right if she goes below with us?"

Harry saw the enthusiasm in the young faces. He had already made a great exception in letting Jamie help his grandfather in the mine. Lee Claybourne had to sign a release form that he was totally responsible if Jamie was accidentally hurt in the mine. Allowing this young slip of a girl to go underground with explosives was just too dangerous.

"Sorry, Windy, but I can't let you go underground with dangerous explosives," he said.

Tears brimmed in Windy's hazel eyes.

"Can we take her down some other time?" Jamie asked hopefully.

"That's a thought, Jamie, but we would need her parents to sign a release that we aren't responsible for her safety," Harry answered, thinking he had solved the problem.

"Ma and Pa are home. Pa can't write too good, but Ma'll write up whatever you want the note to say," Windy said eagerly.

Harry looked at Windy, shrugged, and picked up the phone and handed it to Windy to call her mother.

"We don't have a phone," said Windy, and Harry put the receiver back into its cradle.

"I guess you'll have to wait until you can bring back the permission form with your parent's signature," Harry said as he gave Windy the form to be filled out.

"Will you take us down tomorrow, Grandpa, if Windy brings back the paper?" Jamie asked.

"Sure," answered his grandfather. "Lunch time would be the best as the dust from the blasting will be settled. Windy, can you get a ride up here around noon? We'll meet you here in the office."

"I'll be here at noon if I have to walk," Windy assured him.

The following day Windy arrived before noon and delivered the signed permission slip to Lorraine. In the quiet office, she waited for Jamie and his grandfather to arrive.

Gilbert, the young geologist, showed Windy a map of the mine. "The mine goes down to nine hundred feet and you'll be at Level Five six hundred feet below the surface," Gilbert said, placing his finger on the map where they would be.

"Gee, that's deep!" Windy said.

"Don't be scared," Jamie said as he walked into the office. "It's like riding a big elevator down into the earth."

"I've worked in mines that went a mile deep in South Dakota," Grandpa Lee told Windy.

On the way to the mining shaft, they stopped at the warehouse to outfit Windy for her trip underground. Ernie Wells, the warehouse man, did his best to find a miner's hat that would fit Windy's small head. He took one he could adjust and stuffed it with paper. Then he punched three extra holes in the mining belt so it could be tightened around her tiny waist. Jamie searched through the steel-toed mining boots until he found the smallest pair and stuffed the toes full of paper so Windy's feet wouldn't slide. Grandpa Lee attached a light to her mining hat and hung the battery on her belt. The belt was heavy with the battery and self-contained self rescuer. She was ready to go underground.

"Wow, Windy," Jamie teased. "You could win first place at a Halloween party."

Windy laughed with the others, clumping noisily as she walked and constantly adjusting the hat to keep it from slipping over her eyes.

Grandpa Lee helped her climb into the high four-wheel-drive explosives truck. She was light as a feather.

"Pa says this is a young mine. Is that so?" Windy asked.

"Consolidated Mining has been working the Eagle Mine for nigh on seven years. There are good ore veins throughout this whole mountain. Gilbert says the deeper core drillings are showing a higher grade of uranium. The mine can last another ten years. But you never know, depends on how many nuclear reactors are being built and nuclear weapons." His grandfather's voice held the sad knowledge that uranium could be a friend or a foe, depending on how it was used.

Windy let out her breath at all this new information and shoved back her slipping mining hat. "Pa never told me this mine was so big. All he ever said was that it sure was different from coal mining. He said it was like a honeycomb, full of tunnels with roofs as high as fifteen feet in some places. Not like the coal mines where some of the coal seams were only three feet high. Poor Pa. The seams were so small he had to work on his belly at times. He didn't work for the big mines with modern machinery," Windy explained.

"Do you have methane gas explosions? Some of our friends were killed in coal mine explosions," said Windy as they drove up to the mineshaft and parked the explosives truck.

"We don't have methane but we have radon gas which can cause lung disease. And a roof fall-in at a copper mine killed my dad. They're careful here and roof-bolt where the rock is weak," Jamie informed her.

"What's roof-bolting?" asked Windy.

"That's when the miners drill long iron shafts into the roof. The shafts have collars that hold an iron grid that looks like chicken wire. It holds the weak rock in place," Jamie explained.

Grandpa Lee listened to their conversation in contented silence, happy that Jamie had made a friend who had a quick mind and was full of curiosity. It was hard to believe this was the same boy who, only two months ago, while still grieving for his dad, hardly spoke.

Grandpa waved to the hoist man, Joe Sheepshead, who operated the cables to the cage. The leathery-faced Navajo signaled back for them to come to the hoist room.

Ore Train

Chapter V
EXPLORING UNDERGROUND

It was too noisy to talk above the sound of the air compressors, so Grandpa Lee signaled both of the children to follow him to the hoist house. Windy was sure Joe Sheepshead, the middle age Navajo, wasn't going to let her go underground; but Joe gave Windy a friendly smile.

Joe, with a twinkle in his eye said, "Who's this you're taking down today?"

"Jamie's friend, Windy. Billy's kid," replied Lee.

"Oh," said Joe, with a knowing look. "Can't go underground without your brass tag, little Bilagáana."

"What brass tag?" asked Windy, fearing she wouldn't be able to go. "And what was that funny name you called me?"

"Stop teasing her!" protested Jamie. "Bilagáana is what Navajos call us Anglos. And everyone that goes underground has to wear a brass identification tag."

"Well, Windy, we'll find you a special brass tag. Remember, I control all the gears to the cage and the ride down isn't for sissies," Joe said, giving Grandpa a wink.

"She won't be scared," assured Jamie.

"Okay, Jamie. For your li'l friend's sake I'll give you a slow and easy ride to the center of the earth. Give her brass tag number one, the one for important visitors," Joe said, his black eyes flashing with good humor.

Windy followed Jamie and Grandpa to the mine shaft, trying not to stumble in the over-sized boots. Air whooshed up from the mine below and the thick black cables screeched as the empty cage started its long journey upward to the top.

Windy looked down the shaft for the cage but all she could see was a black hole, lined with rusty ladders, disappearing into darkness. Finally she saw the cage emerge from deep in the earth and stop in front of them. She started to shake and hoped Jamie wouldn't detect her fear.

"Sorta scary the first time," Jamie said, noticing Windy's tense expression. "But I think it's fun. Like a carnival ride."

Windy gave him an anxious look as she entered the cage. Lee latched the wire door and pulled the chain to the bell to signal to Joe that they wanted to go to Level Five. When the bell rang in the hoist room, Joe began lowering the cage slowly for Windy's first ride.

They dropped deep into the earth. As the light above faded into a tiny speck, Jamie and Grandpa Lee turned on their cap lamps. Windy did the same and looked to Jamie for approval.

"Don't look directly at anybody with your light turned on," Jamie cautioned. "Miners can't see when the light shines directly in their eyes."

Windy tilted her head back to look up the mine shaft. The sunlight was a tiny dot fading away as they descended in the darkness. She felt the pressure of the descent in her ears and could hear the great cables groaning. Damp cool air, smelling of earth and diesel fumes, rushed up from the depths of the mine. It felt like air conditioning after the hot desert sun.

"Are you sure the cables will hold?" Windy asked in a quivering voice.

Jamie broke out in laughter as his grandfather pulled the cord to ring the bell. Hearing the bell, Joe stopped the cage at Level Five.

Windy stepped out into a cavern. Dim lights covered with wire mesh gave the tunnel an eerie, hazy glow. Tunnels went off in different directions and faded into darkness.

Windy watched in fascination as a tiny light approached from one of the tunnels. As the light grew larger, Windy could see the outline of a diesel engine pulling ore cars slowly up the tracks. A large miner jumped down from the diesel engine. Mick said to Lee, "Bout time ya got here."

Poking his face into Windy's, he asked, "Who does this sliver of a gal belong to?"

Windy squirmed from the attention and looked down the tunnel.

"Mick, she's Billy Bassett's girl, Windy," answered Lee. "Windy, this is Mick Kelly, the mine foreman."

"Well, I'll be! Looks like Jamie found himself a gal," he teased. "You gonna show the mine to her, Jamie?" Jamie's face turned red and he was glad it was dark.

"If you get into trouble down here, Windy, we'll put you into the penthouse with all the miners," Mick warned with a grin.

"Windy, don't worry, Mick's always joking around. The penthouse is the lunchroom. Remember, Mick's kids told you about Dynamite George?" Jamie explained.

Windy's sharp chin stood out stubbornly and she replied directly to Mick, "Don't worry. I won't do nothin' wrong underground. I'm no sissy! I came all the way down that dark shaft in that cage without being scared at all!"

"Windy, you get up on the engine with me, and we'll give you a short tour of this level of the mine," Mick said, helping Windy aboard the narrow engine. Jamie and his grandfather climbed into an ore car. Mick drove the diesel engine down one of the long black tunnels. Suspended by hooks and wires from the roof were monstrous drooping yellow air vent bags. They heaved and lurched like great yellow worms as a house-sized air compressor brought fresh air from the surface into the mine.

"Do you hear them drilling?" Jamie asked Windy. In the distance they could hear a sound like a machine gun firing underwater. The sound grew louder as the train rattled down the tracks. As they came closer, Windy covered her ears.

They stopped near a drift where miners were drilling with a jack leg drill. Windy trembled with the impact of the bone-shattering vibration; it felt like a locomotive running through her. The noise became even more intense as they climbed up the drift to a point where the miners were working on rock at a dead end.

One of them was Three-fingers Ralph Hall, who, like so many miners, had lost fingers in a mining accident underground. At the end of the drift, he and Skinny Wren, who had long birdlike legs, were drilling the face, a dead end wall of rock.

"The place the miners are drilling is a face," explained Jamie. "The two-inch diameter holes will be loaded with Prell. Then the blasting caps will be attached to fuses that are spliced together to blow the ore vein from the face."

Skinny Wren handed Three-fingers a new drill bit. The bit was taller than either man, both of whom were over six feet. Three-fingers used a monkey wrench to remove the old bit. Placing the new carbide tip bit in the jack-leg drill, they prepared to drill again. The jack was set on a tripod base, so it was easy to angle up, down, and sideways as the miners drilled.

The drill, powered by compressed air, could chew a two-inch diameter hole six feet deep in two minutes. A stream of water going through the drill cooled the bit and helped control the dust. The mist from the drilling created a thick yellow fog and the miners' cap lamps shot hazy searchlights through the choking air as they worked.

The noise was like being underneath a coal train with a hundred cars, thought Windy. Three-fingers wore earmuffs attached to his mining hat and Skinny Wren used foam earplugs that looked like cotton stuck in his ears.

Lee noticed Windy holding her hands over her ears and produced some foam earplugs for Windy, Jamie and himself. Windy sighed as the earplugs muffled the sharp, loud, machine gun sounds. She remembered her Pa saying the sound from drilling destroyed the miners' hearing if they didn't wear proper protection.

Three-fingers' wet gear was spattered with mud from drilling and sweat made rivulets run down his muddy face. To finish the last of thirty holes, he had to reach high above his head. His shoulder muscles were knotted from exhaustion and his hands were stiff from the vibration of the drill, even with the protection of thick rubber gloves.

Three-fingers removed his respirator and spat a stream of tobacco juice, taking a break from the tiring work. Skinny Wren then turned his attention to the wisp of a girl, sloshing awkwardly in her over-sized boots and pushing her mining hat up from her eyes. A gentle smile crept over his mud-streaked face.

"Whatta ya doing down here, gal?" Skinny Wren shouted.

"I want to see where my Pa works," she answered. "And he says the drill weighs a lot and he really gets tired from the work."

"Weighs about a hundred-twenty-five pounds," Skinny Wren bellowed between squirts of tobacco juice. "'Bout two times as much as you."

"You better set the caps and blow the face after lunch," Mick advised. Jamie, Grandpa Lee, Skinny Wren, and Three-fingers jumped ore cars behind the engine. Windy climbed up onto the engine with Mick. Mick started the diesel engine and headed the train toward the lunchroom, near the main shaft.

"Time for lunch!" Mick shouted as he stopped the diesel engine in front of a wooden door marked Penthouse. The door swung open to reveal a small dark room with rough wooden tables.

"Where's your lunch, gal?" kidded Skinny Wren as they entered. "You gonna be down here with us, you gotta bring your lunch bucket."

"Do you eat all your lunches here?" Windy asked, crinkling her snub nose and watching more miners enter through the wooden door. The one lone light bulb that dangled from the roof swung each time the door opened.

"Better than Level Seven where we sit on muddy rocks, in all that water," a miner answered, chewing with big yellow teeth on a roast beef sandwich. "Here, have a Twinkie, our favorite underground dessert: a deluxe cream-filled cupcake."

"Yep, soothes the dusty scratchy throats," laughed Mick.

"Why do you all chew tobacco?" Windy asked, screwing her face up in disapproval.

"Cain't smoke underground. So we chew," answered a muddy-faced miner. "Need our tobacco fix."

"Windy, time to go topside and let these men eat their lunches," Lee said.

"Thanks for the Twinkie. It sure was good after all that dusty air where they were drilling," Windy said. She smiled and waved good-by to the miners huddled around their lunch buckets and mugs of steaming hot coffee.

Returning to the cage, Windy, Jamie, and Grandpa Lee stepped inside. Lee pulled the chain signaling to go up. Windy watched as they moved quickly up the dark shaft toward a speck of light that grew into a blue sky. When they stopped, Lee unlatched the door and they stepped out into the brilliant sunshine. Windy squinted, blinded for a moment.

With her first breath of fresh air, Windy felt reborn. A hot desert breeze embraced her with warmth. She took a deep breath and her tense muscles relaxed. She thought of the cool damp mine directly beneath her feet.

"What do you think of being underground?" asked Jamie.

"Unbelievable! Just unbelievable! It's another world, Jamie!" Windy replied.

She looked at the sun and realized how quickly the morning had passed. She thought of her Pa who worked at nights, and the other miners who worked underground from dawn to sunset in the darkness, never seeing the light of day.

My Pa works in a scary, dangerous world where there is only night and no day. No sunshine, no fresh air, Windy thought sadly. She felt a great sympathy for all the miners working underground.

I'll always be in the sunshine and fresh air, on top of the earth, not inside it, she vowed to herself.

Change Room
Baskets

Chapter VI
NOTHING IS SAFE

The rest of the summer passed quickly for Jamie and Windy. When Jamie wasn't helping at the mine, he and Windy explored the desert. In the evenings, when the fiery red sunset went down in the west, they returned to the log cabin. Jamie would empty Grandpa Lee's old munitions bag of sweet water agates, pieces of flint and other samples he found. Both talked at the same time, eager to tell his grandfather about what they saw through his old World War II binoculars. They saw great Golden Eagles drifting on the wind currents, antelope with their twin babies, coyotes, jack rabbits, prairie dogs, and many other creatures.

They also frequently visited Dynamite George. He had become so tame he would climb on Windy's shoulder and hide underneath her long hair. After a large meal of peanuts, he would sit on Jamie's lap and clean his long whiskers and take his paws and groom his body.

The time to start school arrived. Jamie and Windy both resented having to start a new school and missed their frequent trips to the explosives magazine to see Dynamite George.

When Windy and Jamie stopped coming for their frequent visits, Dynamite George became restless. The nights were turning cold, and frost was on the food he gathered. His instincts forced him to go out each night to gather large stores of food to prepare for winter. He gathered hay, piñon nuts, mushrooms, and dried seeds as well as anything else he found at the mine to carry back to his nest.

Stories about Dynamite George's nightly raids spread like a prairie fire throughout the mining town. The miners talked about the thieving pack rat as they drank their coffee in the mornings and when they met after work in the evenings for a beer at the Broken Spoke Restaurant.

"Yep, I tell you, no matter what Mick says about that pack rat being a kid's pet, he's gotta go," complained Sparky, the electrician. "That critter took my best pair of small needle nose pliers when I was working on wires in a starter at my bench. All I saw was a flash of something — and whoosh, the pliers were gone!"

"Well, you know the kid does try to bring back our stuff," one of the miners answered.

"He ain't done no harm. Just a nuisance. More fun talkin' about a pack rat than what's happening on Level Seven," interjected Skinny Wren.

Windy's father sat glumly off in a corner listening to the men. "These hard rock miners are soft when it comes to brains. Everybody knows no rat has any business in a mine," he muttered out loud to himself.

Billy reflected on his life working in a small West Virginia coal mine. He had worked lying on his belly all day long in a cramped three-foot coal seam, choking and covered with coal dust. Then, as if that wasn't bad enough, he got laid off.

In hard economic times, coal mines laid off hundreds, and William Bassett was just one of the unemployed. He tried to find work for a whole year before he finally gave up. It was hard but, like lots of men, he'd had to leave his family behind to find employment. He'd come tramping out west and landed his job at Consolidated Ores.

The hard rock miners kidded him about his West Virginia accent and hillbilly ways. He put up with it. At least he could put a roof over his family's head and pay for the groceries. Even his sons were working now, and that really helped.

The family vowed never to go through another cold, hungry winter living on beans and corn bread, without enough money to pay the electric bill. He sure didn't want some pack rat upsetting things at the mine and messing up the steady work he and his boys had found.

"That fool rat better not git near my stuff," growled Billy, chomping down on his new upper false teeth.

In the dim light, the miners saw Mick coming through the door of the Broken Spoke. When he heard the miners complaining about Dynamite George Mick stood tall, all his six feet so that his large frame commanded attention.

"The first buzzard who harms a hair on that pack rat is gonna be doing a lot of hurting himself. That pack rat isn't doing any real harm." Mick pulled up a chair and his tone became urgent, "We got some real mining problems. Some union men are here to talk to us about what we can do about Level Seven."

Dynamite George, oblivious to the commotion at the Broken Spoke, was scampering along the edge of the road to the mine in search of anything that appealed to him to add to his collection. A large truck with a load of ore drove past, missing him by inches. Frightened, he dashed out of its way and bumped into a new building he hadn't explored. His long whiskers fit into the crack under the door and he slipped through to the other side. He entered into a large room which smelled like soap, mud, and wet clothes.

He ran up the foam wall to a crossbeam near the ceiling. He heard noises from the showers and in fear ran across the beam to a loose grate. He slipped through the grate into a box with a running fan. He sensed the blades were dangerous and he stayed in the box looking below. There was no activity – just the sounds of voices and running water. He pushed aside the loose grate, ran down the wall, crossed the cement floor, and hopped onto a bench. From there he ran along the tops of the benches, investigating shirt pockets and zippers. Even better, there were sweaty-smelling socks and clothing stuffed into wire baskets attached to chains hanging from hooks from the ceiling rafters. He didn't miss a thing. Everything was moist and interesting. He jumped up onto the row of sinks, skidded on the shiny surface and sniffed each strong-smelling bar of soap as he went. Hanging on a nail next to a mirror was a real treasure – five grizzly bear claws dangling on a silver chain!

He snatched the chain with his dexterous paws, clutched it between his teeth, dashed across the floor, and disappeared beneath the crack in the door.

It was Woody Douglas's bear claw chain, which he always wore with pride. He had shot the raiding grizzly with a 30/30 rifle on his father's Montana ranch when he was only fourteen years old. He loved to tell the story of how it took three shots before the charging bear finally dropped right in front of him. The chain was Woody's most valued possession.

Woody came out of the shower, rubbing his head and body with a towel. He took his clothes from the hanging basket and slipped into them. After he put his boots on he went right to the mirror to put on his chain.

"AAAAAaaaarrrgh!" he bellowed. He grabbed Arnie Nakai, who was drying off nearby, and shook the man violently.

"What'd ya do with my bear claws!" he roared, tossing Arnie against the wall. "You been eyeing my claws ever since you come to night shift."

Crouched and ready for a fight, Arnie's lithe body dodged the next charge. "Not me. Bears are sacred to us Navajo. I wouldn't wear them because they're yours. I admire your claws 'cause I know the courage it took to stand up to a charging grizzly."

"If I find out who snuck in here and took my claws, I'll make bear meat out of them, hear? Just like I did to that grizzly," growled Woody as he stomped off to finish dressing.

The next night, Dynamite George scurried off with Andy McCoy's high school class ring. Andy was the night shift foreman and the only time he took the ring off was when he mined. Andy was a pretty even-tempered person, and he decided they had to figure out who was coming into the shower room and stealing their things.

On the third night, a gold wrist watch was missing. Luigi Houdini went into a rage. It was his watch, given to him by his father; and it had great sentimental value. Tugging at his handlebar moustache in frustration, he screamed, "Any of ya flea-bitten, sneaking coyotes want to die?"

"Somethin's going on for sure," agreed Andy, trying to keep the men in order and tempers down. The miners lived with a strong code of trust because they depended on each other for their lives underground. A theft on a shift would destroy their confidence in each other.

"Somebody took my gold class ring too," Andy said.

"My watch was worth more than any class ring," Luigi answered angrily, blocking the exit to the change room. "Pedro and Billy ain't missed anything."

Billy winced, knowing he wasn't one of the pack. Being a coal miner and not a hard rock miner, he knew he would get the blame if he didn't think fast.

"Probably that dang rat you hard rock miners are so sweet on," Billy said defensively. "Find the rat and look in his nest, then you'll know who stoled yer junk."

Dynamite George, holding his head high, carried his new prize up the mountain by its gold spiral band. The face of the watch banged against the rocks until finally the glass shattered. His whiskery nose investigated the small bits of glass and then, with a firmer grip, he clutched the wristwatch again and continued on his way up the mountain to his nest.

Mick noticed a haze around the fall sun when he drove up Sheep Mountain to the mine. The weather will be changing soon, he thought to himself.

He was surprised to find the night shifters' trucks still in the parking lot. As he walked over to the change building, he could hear laughter. The day shifters were chiding the angry night shifters about the pack rat.

"Ya guys don't have to put up with a thieving pack rat the way we do," hissed Woody. "Mick, we just figured out it was the pack rat stealing all our stuff."

"That pack rat stole my gold watch last night," whined Luigi, knowing that if they found his watch it would never be the same.

"I think the pack rat is raiding us every night and stirring up trouble," agreed Andy.

"We know it's the rat 'cause you day shifters aren't missing anything," Woody growled. "And if you all don't stop hee-hawing I'm gonna smear all of you against the wall!"

"Mick," Luigi complained angrily, "All week things have been disappearing from the change room. We thought someone was stealing from us when we were in the showers. Then last night my Dad's gold watch was stolen out of my pants pocket hanging from my basket."

"No one but that sneaking rat knew your watch was in your pants pocket," smirked Billy.

"I'm gonna go up to the explosives magazine and get my watch back!" Luigi yelled as he shoved open the change room door and stomped toward his pickup.

"Ya can't get into the magazine without Lee unlocking the doors for you," warned Mick.

"I'll get the key from Lee and go up there and get my watch back from that varmint!"

"We're going too!" Andy and Woody shouted, catching up with Luigi.

"We'll all go to the explosives magazine with Lee and check on the nest," Mick said quietly, trying to calm the angry miners.

A group of men crowded into the front seat and the bed of Mick's company truck. They headed out to find Lee. Mick explained the situation to him. Mick and Lee drove the men up the steep road to the explosives magazine. While unlocking the rusty door, Lee saw a flash of gold disappear into a three-foot high nest.

"There he goes!" shouted Luigi. "I swear I saw my watch!"

Lee turned white beneath his whiskers when he saw Dynamite George with the wristwatch.

"Stay out of the explosives magazine!" Mick warned the miners. But they crowded into the small space behind him anyway.

"Lee," Mick said quietly, "let's check out the nest." Lee reached into the three-foot high nest. Startled, Dynamite George leapt out, clutching Luigi's wristwatch between his teeth, and jumped onto the overhead beam with his prize. Sensing danger, he stamped his hind feet, wiggled his pink nose and quivered his long whiskers.

"There he goes, and he's got the watch!" yelled Luigi.

"Don't scare him," warned Lee. "If he gets outta here with the watch, we'll never see it again."

Dynamite George ran along the overhead beam towards a crack above the door, but Lee jumped in front of him. Lee frantically searched his pockets for peanuts and finding one, he crushed the shell and held his hand out to the frightened animal. Dynamite George stopped, tightened his grip on the watch and prepared to spring toward the crack and safety. Lee continued to hold the peanut out, offering it to the small, frightened animal.

For a second, the men froze and watched to see if the pack rat would accept the peanut. Dropping the wristwatch, Dynamite George scurried over to Lee's hand and grabbed the peanut.

Mick went back to the nest and reached deep into the interior. When he pulled out his hand, he held feathers, pieces of antelope hide, candy wrappers and a silver chain necklace with five bear claws. A second reach into the nest revealed a pocketknife, band-aids, a comb, and a high school class ring. No needle nose pliers.

Luigi stood holding his scuffed up timepiece, its hands pointing to 4:55 a.m.

"It's all busted up," he said sadly.

"I'll find you the best watch repairman in Wyoming and get it fixed for you, Luigi," promised Lee.

The men checked out their possessions and left the small room to return to the mine. Dynamite George ran back inside his nest and poked his head out. Before closing the iron door, Lee looked at the animal's perky face and warned, "You're gonna get skinned alive if you don't stay away from the mine."

When the sound of the trucks faded, Dynamite George left his nest and scurried around in the dark, searching in vain for his treasures. By nightfall he would have to head for his favorite place, the change room, to search for new ones.

Chapter VII
ABOUT PACK RATS

Mick's daughter, Fran Kelly, was just out of college, and she wasn't an easy teacher. She had her 7th period eighth grade class working on three projects at once. Jamie and Windy were snowed under with homework. She assigned a five page report about an animal of the Great Basin Desert. The choice was easy for Windy and Jamie and they didn't waste any time in deciding to write their reports about pack rats.

Windy and Jamie met at Grandpa Lee's cabin to write their reports and opened the four nature books they had checked out from the library. They were studying when his grandfather came in with the mail and a small package from the watch shop in Casper. Lee gulped when he looked at the repair bill. He didn't mention the watch to Jamie and Windy. They had the library books opened and scattered on the old oak table to research pack rats.

"Hey, Windy, listen to this," Jamie said, reading from a book on Great Basin Animals. "It says here that pack rats can have two to six babies born in early summer. Due to their secretive habits and native intelligence they have a low death rate." Grandpa groaned out loud and shook his head, thinking one pack rat like Dynamite George was enough.

Jamie continued, "Dynamite George is a Bushy-tailed Wood Rat, *neotoma cinerea,* from the Greek words *neos,* (new), and *temnien,* (to cut), and Latin, *cinereus,* (ashy). His subspecies is *orolestes,* from the Greek words *oros,* (mountain), and *lestes,* (robber). Mountain Robber."

"That's Dynamite George for sure," laughed Windy. "And here's a description of him in this book, plus a photo. It says a pack rat's body is eight to ten inches long and its tail can be five to eight inches long. The whole body can be as long as eighteen inches."

Windy wrote the information in her notebook and then read on, "They are called pack rat, trade rat or mountain rat."

"Dynamite George is a thieving rat!" Grandpa Lee snorted.

"Listen to this," Windy continued. "This subspecies of wood rat is noted for its silky fur, four-inch-long whiskers and large ears."

"Radar ears," Jamie chuckled, "and I think Dynamite George's whiskers may even be longer than four inches the way he twitches them when he's excited and smells peanuts."

"Pack rats are usually vegetarians but have been known to eat meat," added Windy.

"Probably some poor miner's store of venison jerky," Grandpa Lee said.

"Wow, listen to this!" exclaimed Jamie. "It says pack rats are the oldest known paleon-tol-o-gists or however you say it!"

"What's that mean?" Windy asked.

"Something to do with studying old fossils and bones," Jamie explained.

"Like studying dinosaurs?" Windy asked.

"Yes," Jamie responded and continued his reading. "It says here the outer nests of a pack rat are made of loose twigs and sticks to protect the inner nest. They've been carbon dated as far back as 39,000 years ago. To protect their nests, pack rats perch above them and urinate on the branches and sticks, giving the nest a strong musky smell. The urine makes a substance called amber wrap, which cements the nest together and preserves it. In some nests they've found extinct plants and small sloth bones that are over 11,000 years old."

"I didn't know pack rats were that old," Windy said in surprise. "And Dynamite George isn't that messy. The inside of his nest is clean."

"There is a strong turpentine piñon smell, near his nest," Jamie answered. "But it is hard to detect over the strong smell of the explosives."

"He's always sitting on the beam above his nest and probably does leak onto the twigs and branches," Windy commented.

"It doesn't smell bad," Jamie answered defensively. "It's like sticky piñon sap."

"Give him time," his grandfather grumbled.

"Here's more information and a picture of the Desert Wood Rat. It doesn't have Dynamite George's bushy tail, only a few thin hairs. It's a smaller version called *neotoma lepica* and it lives in southwestern deserts," Windy said holding the book up to show Jamie the picture.

She thought about how pleasant it was to come to the cabin in the evenings and study with Jamie. Ever since school started, she'd been coming over to do her homework at the Claybourne's. She enjoyed the walk out to the old ranch. The stars were so bright she could see the dirt road and fences clearly outlined against the hills. The smell of juniper and cedar logs burning in fireplaces filled the crisp night air and she could hear her footsteps crunching on the frozen road. In the cold silence, echoes could be heard off in the distance and, occasionally, coyotes would start their yipping in a chorus. Windy looked through the cabin window at the warm light with a dreamy expression on her face. She looked up at the hypnotic blinking light on the mine tower.

"You O.K, Windy?" inquired Grandpa Lee.

"I really like coming over here to do my homework," she told Grandpa Lee. "If one of the twins ain't moving my books off the table, the coon dogs is chewin' on them, or Daddy's usin' up my notebook paper to start a fire in the barrel stove. It sure is a relief to study in a place where everything ain't so crazy," she said with a smile.

"I'm getting used to Grandpa's cabin too," Jamie said thoughtfully.

"It's cozy like Grandma's cabin in Possum Holler down by the crick," Windy replied.

Grandpa Lee smiled to himself as he looked at his grandson's curly red head, a sharp contrast to Windy's straw-colored hair. Ever since school started, the log cabin had been full of eager chatter about their homework and their great plans for the future.

Saturday Clarabelle struggled to climb the steep mountain road to the explosives magazine. According to Lee, old Clarabelle was once famous for passing everything on the road during the toughest of snowstorms. But that weekend she had trouble making it to the explosives magazine from the cabin. Not only was the clutch badly worn, but the rear axle was making a clunking noise. Grandpa Lee was afraid one of these trips to the explosives magazine would be the last. He didn't have the heart to disappoint Jamie and Windy, as they looked forward all week to seeing Dynamite George.

Jamie shook his head at the sound and told his grandfather that a brand new four-by-four would make a good replacement for Clarabelle.

Grandpa Lee again reminded Jamie he was still trying to pay off their small ranch near the mining town.

"But Grandpa, we got Dad's insurance money. Can't we use it for a new truck?"

"How many times I gotta tell ya, Jamie, that money is for your college education," his grandfather answered and stubbornly stuck out his whiskered chin. There was no more to discuss.

"But I'm going to be a miner, Grandpa," Jamie answered, knowing his grandpa wasn't getting the message. It was a sore point with Jamie, who could imagine driving a loaded truck with a roll bar, big whip CB antennas, and over-sized tires.

"Your dad wanted you to be a mining engineer, son. And you will be one," said Grandpa Lee. "A mining engineer will never be out of work."

"My Pa lost his job in the mines when they shut down," Windy added.

"Windy, man will always be digging at the earth 'cause he can't live without mining and its resources. Someplace in the world there is always a mining job," stated Lee.

As they approached the explosives magazine, a cool fall wind scattered leaves across the road. The vegetation in the desert below looked brown.

Jamie hopped out of the truck with Windy right behind him and they waited for Grandpa Lee to unlock the iron door.

Dynamite George came out of his nest as a shaft of light illuminated the nest and his great store of winter food. Jamie and Windy knelt down with their offering of peanuts. The pack rat grabbed the peanuts and ran up the rough-hewn wooden beam to a corner and placed the peanuts in a neat pile.

"Grandpa, he's storing peanuts instead of eating them," observed Jamie.

"Winter is around the corner and his instinct is telling him to store and gather all the food he can before the snows," his grandfather answered.

"He's so fat now from being fed peanuts all summer he could live off his fat all winter," Jamie added.

Jamie checked out Dynamite George's store of piles of dried grasses, seed heads and clusters of tasty flowers withered on the stalk by the summer sun. He remembered reading for his report that the musty smelling lichens were full of protein, the mushrooms had trace minerals and the piñon nuts were full of carbohydrates.

Dynamite George finished gathering the last of the summer grasses. He'd crawled up the rough wooden wall, legs spread out like a spider, using his sharp toenails for climbing spikes, and placed each strand lightly on top of the heaps of hay to prevent molding. It got to the point where he had to pick a path through the stacks of drying hay to reach the second door. The chilly fall winds were starting to blow through the cracks of wood and under the iron door into the explosives magazine. Dynamite George started chinking the cracks with bits of rags and paper to cut down the cold air.

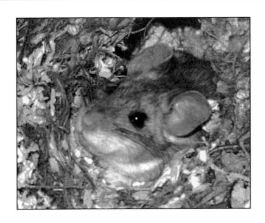

Chapter VIII
BLIZZARDS ARE DEADLY

The trailers of the mining town shook violently as the winter's first blizzard lashed out at the flimsy structures.

Windy pulled on her thin jacket and zipped it up to her chin as she prepared to leave the hot, crowded trailer. She thought walking through the storm to visit Jamie at the ranch would be a relief from all the noise and the bickering twins.

"You cain't go out in that wind and snow, Winifred!" Melanie Anne warned her daughter.

"Gotta go over to Jamie's and do my homework, Ma. It ain't even a mile away," Windy said. As she left, a violent wind slammed the door against the trailer.

She tucked her chin against her chest and leaned into the freezing wind. She started running down the road between the trailers towards the ranch, the wind stinging her face with a mixture of dust and snow.

When she reached Tramp Row, she found great gaps where the trailers belonging to itinerant miners had been parked. The tramp miners had left for the south to mine in Arizona before an early winter. The snow came in blinding sheets carried by winds that lifted Windy off her feet. This was not the quiet snow she remembered in West Virginia, but a vicious swirl of icy daggers that stung her face and took her breath away.

She ached from the cold and it didn't take long for her to change her mind about going to see Jamie. As she turned to go back home, all she could see was a faint glow of lights from the mining town. Her fingers and feet were numb, and the tears, which spilled from her stinging eyes, froze on her cheeks. Gasping against the wind, she fought her way back to her family's trailer.

When she opened the door, the wind blew her inside.

"Shut that danged door," bellowed her father. "You ain't got any sense to go out in a blizzard on foot." Windy glowered at her Pa and struggled to get the door closed.

Melanie Anne came over to Windy and felt her cold hands and cheeks. "Mercy sakes, child, it's much colder out there than I thought. Never in my born days have I seen such wind and snow!"

Melanie Anne led her shivering daughter to the warmth of the kitchen and a heated kettle of water on the stove. "Gittin' you some hot chocolate to warm your innards."

"Thanks, Ma," Windy answered weakly. "Never heerd tell of snow like this. 'Bout plumb blew me off my feet."

Wrapping a shawl around Windy's shoulders, Melanie Anne warned her husband, "Billy, I don't want you going up that mountain tonight."

"The mine'll be working," answered Billy, staring gloomily out of the window at the storm. "Mining never stops on 'count of a little weather."

"But it's not safe for you to go up that steep road when you cain't see!" Melanie Anne answered in a tense voice.

"Annie, if I don't show up tonight those hard rockers will taunt me to death about a coal miner being afeared of a little snow."

"Plumb dangerous to go up that mountain tonight," Melanie Anne repeated, shaking her head.

Windy took the steaming cup of cocoa from her mother. Slurping it gratefully, she stared through the window at the swirling snow. The T.V. antennas on the trailers whipped back and forth in the gale and slivers of cold air leaked through the window frames and under the doors of the shuddering structure. Wind gusts of 70-80 miles-per-hour rumbled the aluminum trailer roof. She heard the old tires used to weight down the roof slide towards the edge.

Still shivering from her first experience with a Wyoming blizzard, Windy tried to shut out her noisy family. She knew that Dynamite George was safe, but she wondered what the other wild animals were doing for shelter in this storm.

Would Jamie figure out that she couldn't see through the blizzard to reach the ranch?

Windy continued to watch the blizzard and sip her hot cocoa. Her warm breath formed frosty patterns on the wintry windowpane.

Meanwhile Jamie gazed out of the cabin window, wishing he had a phone instead of the CB scanner. All he could see was a blank wall of white as the wind and snow blew against the windowpane. Windy wouldn't be able to see a foot in front of her, he thought. He looked over at his grandfather, and thought maybe they could drive over in Clarabelle and pick Windy up. But Grandpa Lee had already taken his boots and his coveralls off. He was sitting with his feet propped up, reading near the warmth of the cook-stove. Jamie knew that even a blast of dynamite wouldn't take his grandfather's attention away from his Louis L'Amour western.

"Grandpa, I don't think Windy can find her way to the cabin in this storm."

Grandpa Lee nodded in agreement and kept on reading. The log walls of the cabin rumbled from the impact of the wind.

"Wow, this is worse than any sandstorm in Arizona! Grandpa, Windy might get lost out there."

Lee shook himself loose from his book and peered over his eyeglasses at his grandson. He reminded himself that this was Jamie's first Wyoming blizzard.

"Don't you worry none about Windy. She won't go out in this storm," his grandfather said knowingly. "I want you to keep an eye on that thermometer for me."

Peering at the thermometer on the outside of the window, Jamie gasped. "Grandpa, you can see the mercury dropping. And come look, it's snowing sideways!"

"You're seeing your first Wyoming blizzard. I'm glad I'm not on swing or night shift. Only fools and desperate men go out in this weather," Grandpa Lee added, with a sigh of relief.

"You mean night shift will go up Sheep Mountain in this storm?" Jamie asked in surprise.

"What'd I tell you about me and Clarabelle in low gear passing all those fancy four-by-four trucks—in the worst blizzard I've ever seen. But the mine kept working. Mining never stops."

"How will they get up that steep road?" Jamie asked in a bewildered voice.

"Snowplows will be out all night clearing the roads and building up snow banks along the edges of the road."

"Grandpa, it's already 20 below zero!"

"And the wind chill factor probably is sixty below," chuckled his grandfather. "You be sure to wear them long-handled I got for you in Lander when you go to school tomorrow."

"Grandpa, the school won't be open!"

`"Oh yes it will, and you're goin' too. A little weather doesn't stop us natives."

68

The wind blew Dynamite George's paper and rags away from the bottom of the iron door. Fine snow drifted into the room and turned it into a small freezer. Dynamite George awoke, shivering. He jumped from his nest to the opening in the vent and poked his nose out into the icy air. The wind lashed at his long black whiskers and the gusts blew him off balance. Desperately cold, he scurried around the room gathering the bits of paper and cloth that the wind had forced out of the cracks. With his dexterous paws, he shoved the pieces of material back into the cracks under the door. Next he climbed onto the oak beams to gather up mushrooms, pieces of hay and piñon nuts which he diligently packed into the warm interior of his nest.

After rearranging his collection of rags, bits of fur and feathers, he ate until he was full and satisfied. On this night Dynamite George wrapped his bushy tail tighter than usual around his body and slept uneasily, awakening to sounds of the wind snapping frozen branches off the trees.

The blizzard raged into the middle of the night. Beyond Dynamite George's hideaway, other creatures were weathering the storm too, finding their shelter in gulches, squeezing under rock ledges, huddling up in caves or burrowing deep into the hollows or roots of trees. Prairie dogs slept deep underground, unaware of the six feet of snow accumulating on the earth above them. Deep in their burrows, cuddled together for body-warmth, they were in a deep sleep waiting for warmer days.

As the storm passed, it left behind a landscape of wind-sculpted snowdrifts. Winter had arrived in Wyoming.

When dawn came, the winds stopped howling, and returned to the normal everyday gusts of a Wyoming winter. Before daylight, the roads were alive with the roar of snowplows as crews worked quickly to remove five foot snowdrifts.

In the vast whiteness, school buses, like large yellow caterpillars, flashed their lights as they stopped to collect groups of shivering arctic-bundled children.

Isolated cattle bellowed, stranded in snowdrifts. Pronghorn antelope shook the white snow off their coats as they shoved their way through the breast-deep snow.

At the mine the night shifters were digging out their vehicles in the parking lot. In the desert below, the day shifters were sweeping a foot of snow off their trucks, preparing for the drive up to the mine.

His grandfather was right. Mining never stops.

Jamie was completely winterized in his new long underwear, down parka, woolen mittens, and flashy red Jackson Hole ski hat. He pushed through the powdery deep snow to the main road. His grandfather had been listening to his CB scanner before daybreak to reports of trucks being blown off the road near Casper. But blizzard or no blizzard, school didn't close. The roads were opened.

Grandpa Lee was relieved to see his grandson's red hat disappear as Jamie headed toward town to catch the school bus. At least he wouldn't have to take the boy's razzing about Clarabelle's pitiful starter-sounds, which wrenched the frozen morning air.

"Come on, gal, you just can't let a little cold weather get you down," groaned Lee as he cranked her again.

Mick's new four-wheel-drive Ram Charger moved easily through the snow as he drove up to the small ranch.

There stood Lee, knee deep in snow, with his head under Clarabelle's hood.

"Keep telling you, Lee, that old truck won't run forever," Mick said, shaking his head at the old miner's stubbornness.

"You're going to be late, Lee, trying to get that old heap started," warned Mick, his breath making frosty vapors in the cold morning air.

"All I need is a good jump," Lee answered in a tired voice. "Believe the battery is down."

"Get in with the others, Lee. The road to the mine is a cake of ice and that old truck won't make it, even with a jump."

"Jamie'll give me a fit if he finds Clarabelle didn't make it to the mine," Lee answered, giving up and slamming the truck's blue hood down. With a grumble he squeezed into the back seat of the Ram Charger with the dayshift miners.

"That old army coat is a wreck, Lee," one of the miners said as he moved over to make room.

"Kept me warm during the war and has been keeping me warm for thirty years in this type of weather."

"Can ya believe it was 25 below this morning and Halloween is next weekend?"

"Heard some of the ranchers didn't get their cattle in. Gonna have to drop hay for them."

"Be a few days before horses and snowmobiles can get through some of those drifts."

"The news said the National Guard will drop hay from their helicopters."

"Hey, Lee, when you retire, you'd better raise goats instead of Herefords on that postage stamp ranch of yours," laughed one of the miners. "You'd never get to feed your livestock if you had to get Clarabelle started in weather like this."

Lee's face tightened with irritation. "Clarabelle's lasted me all these years, and she'll retire when I retire," he answered angrily, knowing deep down that his old truck was shot.

The laughing miners quieted as they braced against the fishtailing Ram Charger's climb up the mountain road to the mine, all four tires spinning. Several times it was only the snow bank that kept them from slipping over the edge to the white-carpeted desert below.

As the miners arrived at the mine, heavy equipment was still plowing and dumping small avalanches of snow over the banks. Bundled up like a rag-tag polar expedition, the men spoke of the weather, almost proudly.

"Yep. A Wyoming blizzard'll put the North Pole to shame."

During the day, the brilliant sun at the mile-high elevation warmed and partly melted the powdery surface of the snow, but at night, the temperatures dropped to thirty below, changing the surface to a glassy-hard crust.

Chapter IX
THE MISSING TEETH

The miners, exhausted from the cold, burst through the change building entrance. They shivered as they stripped off their muddy diggers and hung the dripping outer clothing from their suspended baskets. The men dashed into the steaming showers where hot water spewed from the nozzles, thawing their cold bodies. Within minutes the miners, tense and stiff from a night of mining in frigid air, began to relax.

Before Billy entered the shower, he removed his new upper false teeth and placed them in a glass of water on the sink. His mouth hurt and his jaws ached from clenching his teeth while he long-holed in the bitter cold air. He undressed quickly and followed the other men into the showers. He stuck his muddy face into the stream of hot water and let out a sigh of relief.

"The mechanics were supposed to fix the heaters to the air vents tonight. I'd like to see those guys try to work in that arctic gale," growled Andy, the night shift foreman, as he stood in the hot water and scrubbed the caked mud from his hair.

"If they don't get 'em fixed, I'm going back to day shift. The heck with the extra night shift pay," Pedro answered through chattering teeth.

"If they keep working us in that wind tunnel, I'm gonna take down my air bag. Forget their stupid regulations and all that talk about cancer and radon," grumbled Woody.

"Don't do that," Andy warned, shaking the water from his head. "I heard swing shift got caught taking down their vent bags. The radon got real high and it was worse when they had to reconnect the bags and pump that freezing air into the workings."

"Hard to mine when the wind chill factor is fifty degrees below," Arnie Nakai said, sputtering through hot water. "I'm gonna go back to Arizona and spend the winter in my hogan by my potbellied stove. Maybe I'll get warm then."

"Good idea, Arnie," laughed Luigi. "Maybe the medicine man can conjure up enough money for you to pay off that truck and its high tech speakers."

"My truck's got the best sound in Wyoming."

"So you can listen to Navajo chanting?" laughed Luigi.

"We're all in debt up to our necks," Andy quickly interrupted, noticing Arnie's flashing black eyes. "The more we make, the more we spend and pay in taxes. It's endless."

"Yeh, I guess it could be worse," Arnie answered as he tried to untangle his long black hair under the shower head. "We could be mining Level Seven, and my instinct tells me that is poor ground. If we mine in that cold water, we're gonna come out of that level looking like popsicles."

"Heard at the Broken Spoke the other night, all shifts will be working Level Seven, 'cause they found some real high grade ore in the west drifts," Woody said soberly.

"Bad enough to put up with a thieving pack rat on night-shift. If we work Level Seven, we'll be going for a nightly swim, too," Luigi said angrily. "I'm gonna try for day shift and ask not to work on Level Seven. The cold and wet play havoc with my arthritis."

"Good riddance," smirked Billy. "Yer always wearin' fancy watches and washin' with girlish-smellin' soaps like you're some kinda big shot instead of a miner!"

"Why don't you go back to your still in the hills and make your rotgut moonshine," goaded Luigi. "And take them rank barking hounds, that sleep with you and your missus!"

"Pure-blooded coon hounds, they is!" retorted Billy, swelling up for a fight. "Best trackin' and huntin' dogs that ever come to Wyoming."

"Can't you take any ribbing, Billy?" intervened Andy. "You got a chip on your shoulder as big as a support beam."

"Locos. Todos locos," Pedro spat. "At least we're working and getting a paycheck."

"We're getting a paycheck all right," answered Andy. "But sometimes I think we should listen to the union. Maybe we'd get some better working conditions."

"I thought a union would help us out, but management is against it," Luigi warned. "When I worked as a sandhog on the San Francisco Bay Tunnel, all of us were in the union. No one takes the union seriously in this god-forsaken place. You men are too independent and anxious about making a big bonus."

Dynamite George had been inside the explosives magazine for several days, avoiding the deep snow. He tried to make his nest and the explosives magazine warmer by chinking underneath the door with rags and pieces of paper. He became restless and his pack rat nature for exploration took over.

The large snowdrifts on the mountainside covered his trails to the mine. Slipping and sliding on the smooth hard surface of the frozen snow, he instinctively made his way down the mountain.

A gust of wind caught him unexpectedly. His small body tumbled along the hard-packed snow into the deep soft powder beneath a juniper tree. Struggling out of the powdery pocket, he leapt to the low-hanging branches of the tree, braced himself, shook off the snow and cleaned his bushy tail. With his toenails gripping the crusty snow, he jumped back to the slick surface and cautiously made his way to the mine.

The familiar scene he knew at the mine had changed. He had to navigate over the great white mounds left by the snowplows.

He couldn't locate his accustomed routes to the buildings, so he sniffed the cold air for the familiar scents of steam and diesel fumes. Because his bristling fur created warm pockets of air, he could survive in the extreme cold. However, his pink feet were becoming numb. As dawn approached, his nose picked up the familiar scent of steam mingled with soap and muddy clothes. Skidding over the frozen roads, he dashed in the direction of the smell.

Dynamite George found the building but the crack under the door was covered with an aluminum strip to block out the cold air. He searched frantically for another entrance into the warm building.

As he prowled around the change room, he discovered a crack above in the eaves where steam was escaping. He climbed up the outside of the building and stuck his nose into the steam. With his whiskers as a measuring device, he poked his pink button nose into the crack. The hole was too small. His body wouldn't fit. Dynamite George chomped with his four front incisors on the wet wood and spit chunks to the ground. In an agitated state, he enlarged the small crack enough to tightly squeeze his body through. Frozen and exhausted from the difficult task, he crawled into the cloud of warm steam down to a ceiling crossbeam. He surveyed the area of the change room. His attention focused through the mist to the line of white sinks. His eyes brightened when he saw a shiny pink object in a glass of water on a sink: Billy's new upper false teeth.

Relaxing in the shower's steamy haze and enjoying their harmless banter, none of the miners noticed Dynamite George slyly creeping down the wall into the shower room.

Not to be denied his new found treasure, Dynamite George's glittering black eyes never left the shiny trophy on the sink. Billy's pride and joy had cost the outrageous sum of $775.00. Even his four children knew they would bring down thunder if they fooled around with Pa's new store-bought teeth.

Dynamite George sensed the coast was clear. He sprang to the sink and grasped the teeth inside the glass of water. The wet teeth slipped through his paws and fell into the sink bowl. He pounced on them like a coyote jumping on a prairie dog. Clutching the dentures with his needle-sharp teeth, he jumped to the floor and landed on the cement where one of the front teeth broke loose. He dragged his pink-and-white prize to the foam wall and, with effort, struggled up the wall to the crossbeam. He labored with the teeth until he reached the hole in the eaves. He tried to push them through, but they were too large for the hole. Carrying the teeth, he ran back down the wall to the floor to search for another exit. He was alarmed by the slapping sounds of bare feet approaching from the showers, and his fur bristled in fright.

Without hesitation, Dynamite George clutched Billy's uppers tighter and ran back up the opposite wall to one of the crossbeams. He crossed the slippery beam to his familiar hiding place. He found the loose grate and forced the teeth into the exhaust fan box.

He slipped through the grate and paused to search for an exit by the ice-covered fan. He grappled with the hole caused by the melting ice between the blades and the wall. He gnawed with his razor sharp teeth, spat out small pieces of ice and jerked away larger chunks with his paws. At last the hole was enlarged, but the uppers would not go through to the outside.

Dynamite George was startled by a miner shouting and bellowing in the shower room below. The pack rat stopped struggling with the ice and turned from the fan to peek through the grate below.

It was Billy. Scantily wrapped with a towel around his waist, he started yelling and charging around the shower room. Frightened by Billy's wrath, Dynamite George frantically tore more pieces of ice loose in the fan box. He squeezed his way through the small hole of sharp ice to the outside and scurried down the side of the building. He left his prized possession by the frozen fan blades. In the pink light of dawn, he jumped over the mounds of snow and raced up the mountain to the safety of the explosives magazine.

In the watchman's shed next to the mine entrance, Wyatt, the dozing night watchman, was awakened by the commotion. He bolted out of his chair and stumbled over the logs stacked for the wood-burning stove.

"Someone's being murdered," he mumbled to himself as the ear-splitting yelling boomed from the change building.

He fumbled to draw his pistol and charged out of the night watchman's building into the frozen dawn. "I'm coming," he bellowed.

Wyatt slammed the outer door open and rushed into the change building. "I got ya covered! Don't any of ya varmints move!" he shouted, pointing his .38 Special unsteadily at the half-dressed men, who were holding their stomachs with laughter.

"The first cuss who don't settle down and listen to Wyatt Earp the Third will have to answer to this!" Wyatt roared while leveling his gun at the men.

"Put that cannon away, Wyatt, before you shoot yourself," Woody said, gasping with laughter. "You've been reading too many Westerns."

Wyatt glowered at the miners, who were trying to hold onto their slipping towels as they convulsed with laughter.

"Marshall," smirked Woody, "the only way you're gonna get the outlaw is to shoot him on a dead run."

Snorting like a charging bull, Billy was running in circles. He tried to keep his towel from falling off his skinny red body.

"I know'd it's the rat! I know'd it'd come back, you braying idjits!" His heart was pounding so hard against his ribs, he was sure he would die.

"He took my teeth! My new uppers!" he spluttered, squinting away angry tears.

"Maybe ya jus' mislaid them teeth, Billy," Wyatt said, trying to get a handle on the crisis.

"Mislaid 'em? Mislaid 'em?" shrieked Billy, flapping his skinny arms like windmills. He shoved his face into Wyatt's and shook a fist under his nose.

Ducking from Billy's wrath, Wyatt stumbled back into the wall. As he fell, he accidentally discharged the pistol and the bullet grazed his fancy hand-tooled cowboy boot.

"Put that gun away, ya crazy ole bone picker! Where am I gonna mislay them teeth to? Either they're in my mouth, which they ain't, or on the sink, which they ain't! Or they been stoled!"

A fresh chorus of laughter bubbled up, and the miners started chanting: "Where, oh where, did my false teeth go?"

Turning redder and redder, he pointed his bony finger at Wyatt then spluttered, "I put them uppers in a glass of water on the sink! Right there in the corner! See those tracks of that thieving varmint? Dirty rat tracks all over the sink!"

"Now, Billy, stop howling like a kicked dog or you're gonna drop dead from a heart attack," warned Arnie, trying to stifle his amusement at the cunning trickster's latest raid.

"Don't you warn me 'bout no heart attack! You ain't been skunked by that dadburn rat! I'm gonna get him and skin him alive and hang his hide in the Broken Spoke for all of you to see. Nobody fools with us Bassetts. 'Specially a sneaky rat!"

"Better not skin 'im before you get your teeth back," chuckled Arnie. "If he don't lose them in the snow, that critter will be hauling your teeth back to his nest like he did Luigi's watch. Maybe he'll trade them for something better on the way!"

"Billy, don't you worry none. I'll get holt of Lee Claybourne and tell 'im about yer teeth," Wyatt said, trying to soothe the wild West Virginian and get the situation under control.

"I thought old Lee blocked all the holes to this building," Woody said, laughing. "Danged if that critter hasn't out-foxed us again and found another way in here."

Glowering, Billy climbed into his clothes, yanked his parka on and rushed outside. He was so upset he forgot his hat and gloves. As he ran toward the explosives building, he crammed his hands into his pockets to keep them from freezing in the twenty-five-below weather.

Lee Claybourne, ready to start his day shift, unlocked the explosives building door and was startled when Billy grabbed him by the shoulder. "Give me the keys to the explosives magazine," Billy threatened in a sinister voice.

Lee, still out of sorts and moody about Clarabelle's refusal to start in this extreme cold, wasn't about to put up with this banty rooster.

"You lost something?" Lee answered in a firm voice.

"Yer dang right I lost something! MY TEETH!" bristled Billy through his pink gums. "It was that no-good, sneakin' rat!"

"No way anyone can get up that mountain today. Road snowed in," Lee answered impatiently. "We might be able to get up there tomorrow morning to see if George has your teeth. Let's see if your teeth are in the change room."

Oblivious to the frigid weather, the day shift miners started to gather at the change room, forgetting about work. Over and over, a detailed account was told about how Dynamite George had absconded with Billy's uppers. Roars of laughter broke through the morning's brittle cold air.

Mick could hear the shouting and laughter through the closed windows of the mining office. He set off at a lope to see what was happening. As he approached the miners, he heard them taunting Billy.

"Ain't your lil' gal sweet on Jamie and his rat, same rat that stoled your teeth?" a miner teased.

Luigi couldn't resist adding fuel to the fire. "Your teeth will never be the same after banging up the mountainside, Billy. Just like my watch. You're gonna wear a crooked smile and eat lots of peanuts when Dynamite George gets through with them teeth!"

The miners quieted down when Mick shouldered his way to the center of the group. Shuffling their feet in the snow, like rowdy kids caught doing mischief, they waited for his reaction.

"Why aren't you day shifters getting ready to go underground?" Mick asked, eyeing Lee and Billy, who were glaring at each other.

"My teeth, dat's what! You stupid bear!" Billy lashed out.

Exasperated by the coal miner's hot temper, Mick grabbed Billy by his parka collar. "You settle down, Billy. I gotta see that the day shift makes its quota. And that means all of you."

"But my teeth?" whined Billy, struggling in Mick's grip and trying to avoid the blazing green eyes.

"That's enough," ordered Mick, "you night shifters finish dressing and go on home."

The day shifters, heeding Mick's threats, left with silly grins on their faces to change into their diggers. The night crew gunned their cold pickups and hurried down the icy mountain to spread the word at breakfast in the Broken Spoke: That pack rat of Jamie's stole Billy Bassett's false teeth.

Mick released Billy. Standing weak-legged and rubbing his sore neck, Billy moaned to Mick, "Listen, all I want is my teeth back! Took me years to get my new teeth. Lay-off after lay-off at the coal mines. No money until this summer." Swallowing hard, Billy tried to finish. "When I finally got steady work, I bought some teeth," his voice quieted to a raspy whisper. "Then that blasted rat stoled them this morning!"

Billy's voice drifted off in agony as he looked at the white desert wasteland in the distance. He wondered if he'd done the right thing by moving there.

After Lee and Wyatt Earp III searched the change room, they reassured Billy his teeth would be in the pack rat nest. Wyatt, still embarrassed about his actions, was muttering to Lee, "Hunting nothin' but a thieving pack rat."

Feeling all of his 75 years, Wyatt climbed into his fully-loaded four-by-four Jeep Wagoneer. The doors were plastered with Wyoming's "Search and Rescue" emblems. Glad that his nightshift was over, he slowly drove down the mountain road toward town.

Mick turned to Lee and Billy as they watched the day shifters go underground. "Sonny Jones plans to use a small snow plow to start clearing the road to the explosives magazine but it might take two days," Mick informed the miners.

"Ya mean we cain't get up there today," Billy said in a despondent tone.

"They gotta be careful as they can slip off the edge of that steep road in a snowdrift," Mick answered.

"We will have to dig out the snow around the explosives magazine," Lee added. "It will also be waist deep up there."

"Lee, go tell Sonny Jones we hope to get the snow to the explosives magazine cleared off by tomorrow morning. Tell him to scoop up the snow by the magazine door. And tell him not to take any chances," Mick said, stuffing his mouth full of chewing tobacco.

Billy walked dejectedly to his pick up. Would his teeth be in the nest tomorrow, he thought to himself? Or did that dang rat lose them in the deep snow?

Melanie Anne greeted Billy with a hug. "I heard what happened," she said in a gentle voice.

"Dagburn rat stole my uppers," Billy fumed.

"Billy, you jus' stop your fussin," Melanie Anne said, trying to soothe his anger. "We're gonna have your favorite dinner tonight: chicken and dumplings."

"Thanks, Annie. But I'm not hungry and don't plan to work graveyard tonight. Think I'll wait and go up in the morning to see if that rat took my teeth to his nest," Billy said in a beaten voice.

Billy looked through the steamy bedroom windows toward the mine, knowing he had to get some sleep after what happened there. He undressed down to his long underwear and crawled gratefully under the warm electric blanket. Even with his mother's tulip-design quilt on top, he still felt cold and couldn't relax.

All he could think about was the mistake he had made moving the family west, away from their home and people. He thought about what he'd put Annie and the kids through when the mines shut down. He remembered how hard it had been to scratch a living from the eroded rocky land and how there was never enough to eat. He and the boys used to go hunting with the dogs, even when it was illegal, just to put meat on the table.

Now, with a sneaky, blasted rat making a fool of him, he knew he had to do something about all the negative thoughts bombarding him. Unconsciously, he stroked the long silky ears of his cherished hounds with their chins nestled on his bed.

"You know what, fellas? I've been skunked by a rat," he confessed to them privately. "And that Fancy Pants Luigi, who got his watch stoled, laughed the hardest."

As he remembered the scene in the change room, he could feel his anger rising. Even the warmth of the bed and the sympathy of his faithful dogs couldn't stop him from thoughts of revenge.

"I'm gonna skin me a rat. One way or the other. Nobody fools around with us Bassetts. 'Specially a dang flea-bitten rat!"

The dogs drummed the floor with their ropy tails and whined, thinking they were going to go on a hunt.

"No way that rat can carry my teeth up that mountain through the snow to that magazine."

The dogs' tails continued to thump on the floor.

Making a decision, Billy got out of bed and pulled on his old army fatigues and coat. He marched down the narrow hall, determined to carry out his plan.

Billy stomped through the living room and out the trailer.

"Where you goin', Billy?" Melanie Anne called after him.

"Got some business at the Broken Spoke," he growled.

He plotted his revenge against Dynamite George, as he hiked down the narrow snow-covered streets. His eyes squinted from the mid-morning snow's reflection from the sun. Yes, his plan would work.

At the Broken Spoke, he glared across the hazy dining room at the gossiping miners as they slurped down their coffee and chomped their bacon and eggs.

Flossy, the waitress, gave Billy a belittling smile. "Hey, Billy, is it true a pack rat done run off with your teeth?"

Billy gave her a hateful look then turned away toward the phone booth. He heard a ripple of laughter from the miners in the restaurant.

He fumbled with the phone book. It always gave him problems and he had a hard time finding the United States Government listings. Angrily, he flipped the pages, looking for the United States mining agency.

One of the night shifters, heading for home after breakfast, rapped on the phone booth window.

"Hey, Billy! You callin' the lost and found?"

Cursing at the miners, Billy dropped the phone book in frustration and lost his quarter. When he found it, he called the operator for information.

"Ma'am, I'm trying to call the federal gover'mint mining agency near Homestead."

"There's Mine Safety and Health in Green River," answered the operator.

"Please call them for me."

"That will be $1.25 for three minutes."

He fumbled in his pants pockets for change and dropped the coins into the pay phone. His muscles became tense as he listened to the phone ring and waited for an answer.

"This is a recording for the Mine Safety and Health Administration. If you are calling about a mining accident, please call the regional office at 1-800-222-mine. If you are calling about a complaint or mining hazard, please give us your name, phone number and the information after the beep. Thank you."

"We got a bad fire hazard at the Eagle Mine here in Homestead," he whispered, looking around the room. "It's in the explosives magazine."

A rap on the phone booth window startled Billy. With the phone still at his ear, he stared blankly through the glass at his partner, Arnie Nakai.

With a smile Arnie asked, "You calling the dentist?"

Billy shook his head emphatically and hung up the phone.

Arnie's eyes narrowed with suspicion and he wondered what Billy was up to.

"You ain't causing no trouble for us, are ya?" he asked.

"Just taking care of some business."

"Billy, don't you go fooling around with the law and these hard rock miners. That pack rat will show up with your teeth some day. Pack rats have been known to carry a boot off to their nests."

"Not through a mile of snow, they don't," retorted Billy.

"Come on, I'll take you on home. I hear we'll be working Level Seven tonight. We got real problems on that level 'cause old mother earth's spirits have been spooking the miners down there."

Billy forgot about his teeth for a moment. What were these rumors he'd been hearing about Level Seven? Normally, when Three-fingers and Skinny Wren talked about hearing Tommy Knockers on Level Seven, he didn't pay much attention to them. They were just old-timers. But when Arnie Nakai was worried about earth spirits, it was time to listen. Billy had great respect for his Navajo mining partner. He was a good miner and he had an Indian's wisdom about the earth and its animals.

"I think them ol' hard rockers are yellow-belly about some poor ground," Billy muttered as he and Arnie headed out of the Broken Spoke.

"The old-timers call those sounds Tommy Knockers. We Navajos call them bad spirits from the underworld," Arnie said, his face darkening in thought.

Billy, coming from the coal fields, was smart enough to know he'd better pay attention to Arnie's concern. He had to admit there might be some truth to that old superstition about the Tommy Knockers.

"Nothin's going to stop me from filling my quota. But tonight I'm not going up. I'm not taking any more sass from the men," Billy said, trying to sound macho.

"Then I sure hope you didn't sic the feds on us about the pack rat," Arnie warned. "You've never been here for an inspection. No way can we meet our quota when the inspectors are nosing around."

Billy swallowed hard and his Adam's apple worked up and down his tightening throat.

"No thieving rat's gonna cross William Bassett!" he answered hoarsely.

"Forget about the pack rat. Let's go. You'd better get some extra wool socks and thermal underwear and new diggers at the warehouse today to work Level Seven. It'll be wet and freezing."

"Cain't put any more on my charge over there, not even for new diggers. Old ones will have to do. Me and the boys have been saving to get a four-by-four. Nothing fancy like yours. We can barely make it into Lander in that old van of ours," Billy answered. "Then that fool rat stoled my teeth," he fumed.

They got into Arnie's metallic silver four-by-four Ford Ranger. He knew his buddies on the reservation envied his truck with its white fiber glass shell, oversize knobby all-terrain tires, eagle feathers dangling from the rear view mirror, and Pendleton woven blanket covering the back seat. His twelve-gauge pump shotgun and his thirty-ought-six rifle were visible in the gun rack on the back window.

"If I didn't have my family and my wife's clan to feed, I would go home to the reservation. Also, my truck payments are big," Arnie answered as his thoughts wandered. There was no way he could afford to go home.

The narrow streets of the trailer town were packed with snow. Plumes of smoke puffed into the cold morning air from the trailers.

"Thanks for the lift, Arnie," Billy said.

Jamie and Windy came home early, as the school's furnace quit working due to the extreme cold. In town they both heard the news about Billy Bassett's false teeth. The town kids were having a holiday with the story.

Jamie scuffled with Mick's boys when they teased Windy about her father's false teeth. By the time they got to the Bassett trailer, Windy's face was streaked with tears from all the teasing.

As she entered the family trailer, she saw her father with tight white lips sitting on the sofa. She knew he was angry. His blue eyes had that dark stormy look.

"Pa, it cain't be true—can it . . . that Dynamite George took your new teeth?" she asked anxiously.

"It's true," Billy mumbled.

The next morning Billy stood silently by the door of the explosives building. Tense and white, he waited for Lee Claybourne. When Lee and Jamie approached the shed, Billy rushed towards them and demanded they go right up to the magazine.

Mick came over from the mining office and said it was all right for Bassett to go up to the explosives magazine if the road was clear.

"All I want are the keys," Billy demanded.

"Billy, the keys to the explosives magazine won't help you. Told you yesterday, we need to clear away the snow from the magazine," Lee answered curtly. "Besides, Sonny is still working on the road."

"Billy, you better put on your mining boots as we need you to help us dig out the door when we get up there," advised Mick as he and Lee headed for the explosives truck.

Jamie was glad he was there today. He'd make sure they would find Dynamite George's latest prize. He started chuckling when he thought how funny Dynamite George must have looked carrying the false teeth.

It was easy for Jamie to find Sonny Jones and the snowplow on the road to the explosives magazine. All the boy had to do was listen above the mining noises for the clear beep, beep, beep of the back-up bell on the snowplow. Jamie ran toward the snowplow and waved in hopes Sonny Jones would see him.

Sonny stopped when he saw Jamie hurrying towards him.

"What's going on, Jamie?" Sonny asked, turning down the volume on his country and western music. "Why aren't you in school?"

"Furnace broke down because of the storm so they closed school today," Jamie answered. "Mick says we gotta get into the explosives magazine today as the mine is low on Prell. And we need to find Mr. Bassett's teeth. Dynamite George took them. I bet they're in his nest."

"Yes, I heard about the stolen teeth. I can't believe it," Sonny whooped with laughter. "This is the best pack rat story yet! Boy, fur is going to fly today if they don't find Billy's teeth. Billy's got a hot temper."

Lee, Jamie, Mick and Billy crowded into the explosive truck. Jamie was crammed against his grandfather. The truck followed behind the snowplow through a narrow lane up the steep snow-covered road. Lee tried to ignore Billy's cursing against Dynamite George.

"If you can't shut up, you'd better get out and walk," Mick warned Billy. They followed the snowplow in silence to the explosives magazine. Billy jumped out of the truck and rushed ahead of the snowplow to the iron door. Since the snow was too deep, he gave up and waited for the snowplow.

"He cain't be in there! No way could he get through all this deep snow to get inside," Billy said, shaking his head hopelessly. "Luigi was lucky to get his watch back. Weren't no snowdrifts then. My teeth might be anyplace under this snow on this mountain."

"Don't give up, Billy. Dynamite George always returns to his nest before dawn," said Lee. "See those air vents in the rocks? That's one way he gets in and out."

Sonny plowed away the snow in front of the magazine. He did the best he could to make a path to the door. Jamie and the men took shovels and picks from the back of the pickup to finish clearing the snow and ice away from the rusty iron door.

Still exhausted from his struggles with the teeth two nights before, Dynamite George listened drowsily to the snowplow and the voices. When the men started chipping at the frozen door hinges, he burrowed deeper into his nest, stamping his hind feet in alarm.

Lee, trying to unlock the frozen door, muttered to himself. "Not only do we need a blow torch to open this door, we need one to thaw this confounded lock!"

"Maybe this'll do it," he said, reaching inside his winter coveralls for his pipe lighter.

After thawing the lock with the long flame, he tried the key, and it turned. The three men pushed the large iron door open.

Mick shone his flashlight into the dark interior. The beam of light displayed a huge mound of selected rubbish and hay piled two feet high.

Billy gasped and shoved Mick aside. Charging the nest he started to yell, "Where's my teeth, you thieving rat?"

In a fury, he kicked the nest before Mick could stop him.

Dynamite George leapt up from the collapsing nest, whizzed by Billy's nose and escaped through the door.

"Git 'im! Git 'im!" shouted Billy, following the pack rat out the door and landing in a snow bank. "He's takin' off like a flyin' squirrel!"

Billy, hip deep in a snow bank, quickly gave up the chase and climbed out. He sputtered and cursed as he brushed the snow off his clothes.

Jamie carefully felt inside the destroyed nest for the teeth, but they weren't there. He withdrew his hand, and shook his head sadly. "They aren't here, Mr. Bassett," he choked.

"Gotta be there! Gotta be there!" Billy raged, coming into the small room and searching the area. Hay tumbled off the beams as he frantically felt along the ledges. He searched through Dynamite George's entire winter food store. Not finding his teeth, he kicked the nest again with a vengeance.

"You ain't gonna find your teeth that-a-way," warned Lee. "Leave his nest and food alone."

"Ya crazy ole coot! I'm gonna tear every inch of this place apart until I find my teeth."

"I told you the teeth aren't here, or they'd be in his nest, or his usual hiding places," Lee said, clenching his whiskered jaws, his gray eyes flashing steel.

Mick shoved Billy out of the explosives magazine and cautioned, "The only hope you have of getting your teeth back is to wait for the pack rat to bring 'em back to the nest. If you keep tearing this place up, you'll never see your teeth again."

Billy, dejected, stalked to the truck.

"Let's load the Prell and lock 'er up, Lee," Mick said. "I've got enough problems trying to get the men to mine Level Seven. Can't spend anymore time chasing after false teeth."

Perched in a piñon tree, Dynamite George watched the snowplow and pickup disappear down the road. Only a rowdy jay disturbed the silence as the cold winter wind blew up from the desert floor and whipped at the trees. Dynamite George returned to the shelter of the explosives magazine and timidly crawled through the vent into his ruined home.

Riding down the snowy mountain road, Jamie thought about Windy's dad. Everyone in the mining town knew about his temper. Silently, Jamie turned his head and looked back, wondering if Dynamite George would ever be safe again.

Jamie could feel the tense silence between his grandfather, Billy and Mick. The four of them were uncomfortable crammed together in the front seat of the explosives truck. He moved closer to his grandfather and kept watching Billy out of the corner of his eye.

Chapter X
THE TOMMY KNOCKERS

Quietly—without speaking to anyone—Billy left the mine. He drove down the mountain in a fury. It was noon when he arrived at the trailer. He stomped the snow off his feet and entered yelling, "Annie!"

"Dang rat didn't have my teeth!" he sputtered.

The two coonhounds, sensing trouble, ran over to him timidly, licked his hands and stared up into his face. That did it. His sullen face softened a bit. His hands touched a floppy ear as his nose picked up the sharp, salty smell of frying country-cured ham. His mouth watered.

"Now, Annie, why did ya cut into our Christmas ham for?"

"That ham's for special occasions, Billy," Melanie Anne answered softly, as she lifted a tray of golden biscuits out of the oven.

"But ya know how we carried that ham all the way from home for the holidays," he groaned.

"Billy, you hush and sit down," Melanie Anne said while she spooned ham on a platter. She added flour to the gravy in her frying pan and stirred.

"In the coal mines there ain't rats. Also I'm gonna die of lung cancer working in that uranium mine!" he said, feeling sorry for himself.

"Billy, you ain't going to die of lung cancer. And black lung was getting you bad in the coal fields. Just like your pa," she said, as she took the gravy over to the table.

Windy carried a cup of coffee to her father. "Don't worry, Pa," she consoled him. "Dynamite George always carries back his finds to his nest. They'll show up."

He glowered at Windy, then turned to his plate and poured the gravy over everything.

Billy gummed the tough ham, feeling very sorry for himself. He finished off the biscuits and gravy and handed the last few pieces of fat to the waiting dogs. They gulped down the chunks of fat whole then thumped their big tails on the kitchen floor.

"And we cain't afford another set of uppers no matter how many feet I drill," he said despondently, leaving the kitchen table.

Melanie Anne smiled gently. "Things are getting better, Billy. We lived on beans and corn bread for two years at the old Jack Place when the small mines shut down."

"We ate, didn't we?" he answered defensively.

"We ate. But it was hard in the winter. The children went without," her voice trailed off as she relived the harsh memories.

"Annie, I long-holed night shift all summer to get us out of debt. Then I finally got my teeth. And now that fool rat carted them off. No telling where!" His eyes flashed with anger.

"Musta been pretty fine teeth for Dynamite George to take a liking to them and carry them off," Melanie Anne said in a gentle voice.

It wasn't amusing to Billy. He burped on his full stomach but his eyes softened when he looked at his Annie.

"That was mighty fine fixin's, Annie," he said, leaving for the tiny bedroom with the two dogs at his heels. He turned at the bedroom door and said, "I don't want to hear another word about that rat!"

Windy and her sister, Laura Lou, were listening to their parents in the small living room. The sisters tried to hide their giggles when their mother said how fine the teeth must have been for Dynamite George to steal them.

Melanie Anne called Windy to help clean the lunch dishes. She calmly wrapped up the smoked ham in a cornmeal sack as though nothing had happened. Windy was always amazed at how her mother could cool off her father's hot temper.

At the mine, Jamie was really upset about the missing teeth. He found it hard to concentrate on measuring the fuses correctly.

"I'm going down to Level Seven to deliver a load to the powder magazine," said his grandfather.

"Can I help you?" Jamie asked hopefully. "I've never been to that level."

"No, Jamie. That level is wet and muddy and I don't want you wading through all that water when it's 10 degrees outside," Grandpa Lee answered.

"There you go again, treating me like a baby," Jamie grumbled. "I'm tough. Getting wet and muddy won't kill me."

"All right, get bundled up in some of my old diggers hanging there. That level is full of water and you're gonna get soaked."

Jamie shoved his legs into the over-sized waterproof diggers. He cinched around his waist the belt with the battery pack and self-contained self-rescuer. He put on his hat, cap lamp and rubber boots before helping his grandfather pack the caps and the fuses. Grandpa Lee loaded them into the back of the explosives truck, away from the crates of Prell. He and Jamie drove to the mine shaft, unloaded the crates, and placed them next to the shaft. Lee rang for the cage.

Mick came over and gave Jamie a questionable look and asked, "You going down to Level Seven, Jamie?"

"Helping Grandpa," he answered with determination.

"Colder than a well-digger's arse on that level," Mick growled, "and wet."

"He has to try it all," Lee said, as he packed the last crate of Prell into the cage.

As they got into the cage, Lee pulled the chain and signaled to Joe. The cold air whipped around them as they descended deep inside the mountain. When they approached Level Seven, water started to stream down on them. Almost 900 feet below the surface, unloading the wet crates on the slippery platform became a difficult task. The platform was slippery and it was hard to unload the wet crates.

In the distance Jamie could see the light of the diesel train as it approached, as well as the cap lamp of a miner.

The train car skidded on the muddy tracks, stopping at the platform in front of them. Three-fingers jumped off the engine and helped them load the crates onto the train.

Jamie was so cold he wondered why the dripping water didn't turn to icicles. He climbed aboard with his grandfather and Three-fingers. They started back down the tunnel.

The cold air blasted right through Jamie's diggers and jacket to his bones. He helped unload the crates into the wooden powder magazine. The water was so deep in places, it seeped over the top of his mining boots. His feet made a sucking noise in the mud. No wonder all the miners complained about this level, he thought.

Finally, they finished delivering the explosives. The cage carried them away from the dark, wet world below, into the sunlight above.

Jamie was so numb he could barely climb into the truck. At the explosives building, he ran inside, pulled off his boots and socks and emptied out the water. He struggled to get the slippery wet diggers off. Then he took off his wet winter jacket, his shirt and Levis. Clad in only his T-shirt and jockey shorts, he stood barefooted in front of the wall heater. He turned it on full blast until his skin was bright red.

"Grandpa, that was awful," he said, shivering. "Why does that level have so much water?"

"We are into the underground water tables," his grandfather answered.

He watched his shivering grandson dry himself off and threw him a pair of warm wool socks, an old flannel shirt and some oversized pants, which sagged on the boy's thin frame. Lee took off his boots, diggers and jacket. He was relatively dry compared to Jamie.

"You can go back down if you want," Grandpa Lee said, teasing his grandson.

Jamie shook his head. When he was warm again, he went back to the bench and silently started measuring and cutting more of the orange fuses.

Later in the afternoon, day shift came topside, showered and changed. Three-fingers and Skinny Wren came over to gossip and gripe about the conditions on Level Seven. Lee, an experienced miner, was a good listener.

Jamie was silent and was surprised to hear the fear in the voices of the two grizzled miners.

"Lee, I heard them Tommy Knockers tapping and moaning in the west drift again today. Ain't that so, Three-fingers?" Skinny Wren said in an anxious voice.

"Yeh, we sure heard somethin' all right. I ain't been spooked by Tommy Knockers in years, Lee. But I'll tell you, I'm not going to work in Level Seven tomorrow," Three-fingers said with determination. "Mining down there's got my skin crawlin'."

"That young greenhorn geologist, Gilbert, was snooping around with his geology hammer, tapping the rock and saying it was solid. He says the water is from underground springs and shouldn't be a problem," Skinny Wren said, trying to sound reassuring.

"Humph! He cain't read rock. All of us old-timers can tell that's poor rock and we are now drilling into clay," Three-fingers said, shoving a wad of tobacco into his mouth. He chewed thoughtfully.

"Jamie, when you get yer fancy education in those big colleges, don't you forget about what us old-timers know," Skinny Wren said warmly.

"Grandpa is teaching me everything about mining," Jamie bragged. "I hear about the Tommy Knockers all the time, but Grandpa doesn't talk about them."

"Lee, you mean with a name like Claybourne, you ain't been telling your grandson about the Tommy Knockers? Those wee devils who haunt the mines and play tricks on us miners? Well, Jamie, I tell you, they're bad news," Three-fingers said, tobacco juice trickling down his chin.

"Tommy Knockers cause more devilment than a dozen pack rats," Skinny Wren forewarned.

As the old-timers left, Jamie turned to his grandfather. "Are you superstitious about them too?"

His grandfather's light gray eyes saddened. He tousled his grandson's rusty hair. "Jamie, sometimes I wonder about your dad's accident."

Bewildered, Jamie asked, "What's that got to do with Tommy Knockers?"

"Okay, I'll tell you about it while we drive down the mountain. Get our lunch buckets and put our gear into the truck while I lock 'er up, son," his grandfather said.

It was cold and dark when they left the explosives building and climbed into the truck to start down the mountain. Grandpa Lee was using the company truck while a mechanic in town worked on Clarabelle to install a new alternator and battery.

The road was icy and treacherous. Lee drove slowly, chewing on his pipe and scratching his whiskers. He was unusually serious.

Jamie waited, knowing his grandfather was winding up to tell a story.

"I keep my thoughts about Tommy Knockers pretty much to myself," he began. "My great-grandfather, from the old country, taught us Claybournes his beliefs. There were a lot of old sayings, you know, handed down from generation to generation. Some say they were true. One of them said: 'When a rat runs out of a mine, so does a miner.' And 'Hear the Tommy Knockers knocking. Beware.'"

His grandfather paused as he negotiated a sharp curve in the road. He seemed to be drawing from long-ago memories as he continued, "My great-grandfather was such a good miner, he could smell the ore."

The two of them rode in silence for a while. Then Jamie's grandfather began again, "You know, to this day, I think there was mischief with that roof fall that killed your dad."

Talk of his father's death always jolted Jamie, but he knew gremlins weren't to blame.

"It was 'cause the day shift didn't bar down the roof after blasting," Jamie answered. "Are you saying you think Tommy Knockers caused the roof fall?"

"Son, Tommy Knocker stories go way back to Cornwall, in England. In the 1850's, when the Cornish miners left the tin and copper mines on the moors and came to the U.S., they brought their mining skills and traditions with them," Grandpa Lee told Jamie before continuing on with his story.

"The Cornish miners were called Cousin Jacks. They worked the iron fields of Michigan and then they came west. They mined the biggest vein of silver, the Comstock Lode in Nevada. Our Claybourne ancestors spread out from there.

"Well, what's that got to do with Tommy Knockers?" Jamie asked, impatiently.

"The old-timers say the word 'Knocker' came from the ancient word called 'Nicor,' which means 'underworld fairy.' Now a 'knacker' is an old mining tool, and it makes a tapping sound. When the Cornish miners heard the tapping in the mines, they said it was the 'Tommy Knackers.' Usually happened right before a cave in."

"What do they look like?"

"Old-timers tell me they are hideous, gnarled old men with stringy red hair and peaked caps. They move around in groups, disappearing in smoke when a miner comes near."

"Why do they cause so much trouble?" Jamie asked, grinning slightly at Grandpa Lee's sober expression.

"They are the rulers of the underworld," his grandfather explained, "and miners disturb them."

Jamie looked back up at the mine tower, thinking of his experience in the underworld of Level Seven.

"It all sounds silly, Grandpa," Jamie said, but he wondered. Had he heard any unusual sounds down there? Even Windy told him her father had seen flashes of light dancing in the coal seams. A shiver crept up Jamie's spine.

The truck crunched to a stop in front of the cabin, dark and bleak in the barren snow-covered landscape. No smoke came from the chimney as they unloaded their gear from the truck into the cold log cabin.

"Jamie, hustle on out and bring in more logs from the wood pile so I can get us a good fire built," Grandpa said, while he placed cedar chips in the dead coals in the woodstove. Jamie gathered a few chunks of frozen bark and some cedar logs. He paused for a moment to stare up at the blinking mine tower light. He reflected on the day: the cold underground hell he had visited at Level Seven, and Grandpa Lee's Tommy Knocker stories.

He wondered what Dynamite George could possibly be doing with Billy's false teeth. Well, at least he felt sure that Dynamite George didn't have anything to do with the problems and sounds in Level Seven, even though the miners' accused the pack rat of causing havoc.

As Jamie stumbled wearily back to the cabin, with his arms full of logs, he thought to himself, could they have been the Tommy Knockers the miners heard?

Chapter XI
DYNAMITE GEORGE GOES UNDERGROUND

Dynamite George spent most of the day curled up in a branch of a juniper tree. In the afternoon he timidly returned to the vent and crawled into the safety of the magazine. Twigs, sticks, peanut shells, rags, candy wrappers, were scattered on the floor.

First, with oily rags from the machine shop, he chinked the crack at the bottom of the iron door to stop the frigid air from blowing in. He then scurried around to gather some sticks and twigs to repair the damage to his nest. He lined the interior of the nest with rags and paper before he crawled in and fell asleep.

It was hard for him to stay asleep since he awakened at every sound: juniper tree limbs creaking in the wind; coyotes howling. He listened intently for engines and the crunch of tires on the snow.

Several nights passed as he worked to replace the hay on the large oak beams. He made new hay stacks near his nest and pushed dried mushrooms back into crevices between the large oak beams. Satisfied with his repairs and that his food store was safe for the winter, he crept out to survey the scene below him. The mine tower light blinked hypnotically. In the distance, he saw the moonlight reflected off the snow-covered desert floor. He sensed no danger. He leapt through the snow and started his descent to the mine as he tumbled and slid on the frozen surface.

After he reached the change building, he crawled through his narrow chewed-out opening under the eaves into the shower room. He ran across the rafters to the exhaust fan grate. He pushed the corner of the grate aside and entered. By the frozen iced-in fan blades, there was the shiny new treasure for his nest.

Again Dynamite George grappled with the teeth, but the hole in the ice was too small. He chewed and bit angrily at the ice until he was exhausted.

Suddenly, he heard the voices of the night shifters entering the change building and he poked his head through the loose grate to investigate.

"Didn't I tell ya, they'd have us working Level Seven?" Andy complained angrily, pulling on his rubber overalls.

"Swing shift said the heaters are frozen again," grumbled Luigi, "and that cold really makes my arthritis act up."

"Without those heaters working, that freezing air is like a blast from the North Pole," Woody added, shivering at the thought of working underground in the cold wind.

Dynamite George watched the miners pile on layers of clothing, zip up thermal underwear and pull on rubber, steel-toed boots. To top off their protective covering, they added stiff, yellow wet-gear and mining hats.

Luigi started to pull on his wet-gear when he smelled a whiff of the meatball sandwich in his lunch bucket. "Think I'll eat part of the sandwich Angela fixed for me while it's still warm. It'll be frozen solid in that underground hole by the time I get to eat it."

He opened his lunch bucket and peeled off the aluminum foil. Soon the steamy shower room was filled with the strong aroma of Italian sausage, tomato sauce and garlic.

"Just don't breathe on me tonight," kidded Woody, holding his nose.

Luigi smiled, took three large bites, gulped and gave a satisfying burp. Wiping the tomato sauce off his handlebar moustache, he teased Woody. "You're just jealous 'cause you don't have nobody cooking for you. I'll finish the rest later," he said, placing the partially-eaten sandwich back in his lunch bucket.

Dynamite George's nose and whiskers twitched in excitement when he smelled the savory sandwich. He had been days without anything to eat but hay and dried mushrooms. Cautiously, he poked his head out the grate. His nose followed the strong scent drifting up from a black lunch bucket sitting on a bench.

"Get a move on, men," yelled Andy, as he opened the door. "The cage is waiting to take us to a fancy swimming party."

The miners picked up their lunch buckets and stainless steel thermos jugs and followed Andy out the door.

The pack rat slid down the wall and scampered out behind the miners. He dodged in and out of moonlit shadows and through the piles of snow to keep up with Luigi's lunch bucket. Once at the mine shaft, he stayed well hidden in the shadows and updraft steam. He watched as the miners took their numbered brass tags and prepared to go underground.

Running late, Billy caught up to where the night shifters were huddled. He once again ignored the taunts from the other night shifters.

"We thought you were still up at the explosives magazine trying to skin a rat," smirked Luigi.

"Night shift has already started, Billy, and you've been late the last few nights," Andy warned. "Grab a-holt of those drills and let's go down."

"Let me get my tag," Billy answered, stomping over to the board and grabbing his brass tag. While he helped load the drill bits and equipment, Billy didn't pay any attention to the other men who taunted him nightly.

Neither he nor any of the other night shifters saw Dynamite George jump aboard the cage and hide behind the stacks of equipment and lunch buckets. The pack rat crept out from his hiding place, put his nose against the crack in Luigi's lunch bucket and inhaled the wonderful smell of the meatball sandwich.

Luigi rang the bell to signal the hoistman to begin their descent to Level Seven. As the cage hurtled downwards, the whooshing air created pressure in the pack rat's ears. The miners huddled together, trying to keep the dripping water in the mine shaft from leaking down their collars.

With a glum expression, Andy pulled the cord, signaling hoistman to stop at Level Seven. The water at this depth was pouring steadily over their hats, underneath their collars and down their backs.

The cage jolted to a stop. The men opened the gate and started unloading the equipment. Shivering and wet, Dynamite George jumped off the cage and followed Luigi--and his lunch bucket--to a train. The miners climbed into the train and ore cars and sat huddled together, holding their lunch buckets and thermos bottles in their laps.

The pack rat hopped through the mud and water and followed the meatball scent. He scampered aboard the engine of the train then quickly disappeared under Luigi's seat, next to the lunch bucket.

"Keep 'er going slow," Andy yelled to Pedro, the train driver. "Tracks to the north are partially underwater and covered with mud."

"Yeh, just like when I was a sandhog working on the tunnels in the Bay area," groaned Luigi. "That's the reason I got such bad arthritis. Never thought I'd see the day I'd be working in these conditions again."

"I don't think the big shots in Chicago know how bad it is down here. All they're interested in is their quota," Woody growled. "They forget about the men who have to do the dirty work."

The train jerked forward and splashed through the muddy water. All the way down the main tunnel, water poured off the sides of the ribs and dripped from the roof.

"That greenhorn geologist doesn't know what he's doing, trying to keep this level operating," Pedro complained.

Arnie crowded into a corner of an ore car and kept muttering to himself, "Lots of bad spirits down here. Mother earth says she's tired."

The ore train sloshed its way along the tracks past a large electrical transformer. Compressors on the surface pumped freezing night air into the mine and large yellow vent bags heaved like laboring lungs. They stopped at the powder magazine to pick up crates of Prell, the detonator caps, and fuses before placing them carefully into an ore car.

Ducking the vent bags, Woody and Andy jumped off the train. They climbed up an incline to an opening partially excavated where they were following a vein of ore. They prepared the jackleg drill and began to work on their knees in the small cramped area.

Pedro continued to drive the train toward the west. He stopped the train. Arnie and Billy unloaded the crates of Prell from the ore car. They hoisted the crates onto their shoulders then hiked up the drift to the face they were working.

Pedro moved the engine forward down the main tunnel until he came to a large cavern and stopped at the end where the front-end loaders were parked. Dynamite George, huddled by Luigi's muddy mining boots, was alarmed by all the activity; but the delicious smell of the meatball sandwich was stronger than his fear.

Pedro and Luigi jumped off the ore train. Luigi grasped his lunch bucket and thermos and followed Pedro up one of the drifts. They waded through ruts of muddy water to the end of the drift where they put their lunch buckets safely on some level rocks along the rib. Dynamite George kept up with the lunch bucket as he hopped through the ruts and muddy water.

Luigi, full of mischief, warned Pedro, "watch out for them Tommy Knockers. The swing shift said they heard them groaning and moaning in this drift."

"Just stories, but I'm not afraid," Pedro answered, hooking up the drill to the compressor lines.

At that moment a low groan seemed to filter through the rocks. He gave Luigi a startled look, but Luigi was busy cursing at the swing shifters for taking down the vent bags and turning off the fresh air from the surface.

"I'm gonna hook these babies back up. Swing shift can die of lung cancer, but not me," Luigi said as he hooked the air line to the yellow vent bags and turned the valve on with a large monkey wrench. A blast of freezing air filled the drift. Both miners put rubber plugs in their ears and respirators over their noses and mouths so they wouldn't breathe the uranium dust.

Pedro, now a little spooked, tightened the new carbon-tip drill bit into place with a large-toothed wrench. Even though he had tried to ignore Luigi's prattling, Pedro started to think there might be some truth to those stories.

Dynamite George could see the miners ahead of him, their lights making zigzag patterns on the rock face, as they positioned themselves to drill.

Dynamite George searched for Luigi's lunch bucket. When he found it, he started to pry at the latches; but a blast of cold air from the vent bags blew him off balance. He regained his footing and returned to the lunch bucket. He couldn't open the latches.

Just then the rat-tat-tat-tat-tat-tat sound from a jackleg drill exploded through the air. Terrified, Dynamite George shot straight up in the air and landed in a rut full of water. The thunderous noise continued. It followed him wherever he ran.

Eventually he realized the noise was not a threat and he got use to it. Cold and wet, he was determined to get at the meatball sandwich. He cleaned his wet fur before he scampered back to Luigi's lunch bucket.

He pulled and jerked at the resisting latches with his front paws. Pressing his twitching nose against the crack in the lunch bucket, his large protruding eyes glinted greedily. At last, forcing the latches open with his paws, he tilted back the lid and jumped in. He grabbed the edge of the sandwich, ripped away the aluminum foil and buried his nose into a delicious hunk of meatball.

Luigi hadn't left very much, even for a pack rat. He gobbled down what was left, licked up the crumbs and then sat up in the middle of the lunch bucket to clean his face, ears and long black whiskers.

The machine gun noise continued, and Dynamite George decided to investigate another lunch bucket that smelled like corn. Those latches sprang open easily. Inside he found some pork tamales wrapped in corn husks and prepared by Pedro's wife, Chiquita. He was so engrossed in eating the soft tamale, that he didn't notice when the drilling stopped.

"Madre Mia, I can't take this cold any longer," muttered Pedro through chattering teeth, as he wiped the drilling spray off his face.

"You're right, Pedro. The heck with the quota. Let's get outta this wind and get some coffee," Luigi said, letting go of the jackleg drill sitting on the tripod. "Look at my moustache—it's frozen stiff."

They slopped through the mud until their lights shone on their lunch buckets. They caught the gleam of greedy black eyes and small paws clutching a tamale.

"Pedro, a pack rat's in your lunch bucket!" yelled Luigi, charging toward the surprised animal.

"Bandido!" Pedro bellowed, slipping and sliding towards Dynamite George.

The startled pack rat fled down the drift through the mud and water. Suddenly he froze, one paw poised in mid air, and listened.

His sensitive ears felt a change of pressure in the air, and he heard a rumbling sound coming from the rock. The earth started to vibrate. The stomping, steel-toed boots were almost upon him when he turned. He charged through the miner's legs and ran blindly toward the parked ore train.

"Get 'im!" screamed Luigi. He turned and chased Dynamite George down the tracks. "He's running alongside the ore cars."

Pedro came to a halt, huffing and puffing. He gasped to Luigi, "That pack rat changed directions. When a pack rat runs out of a mine, we should be right behind him!"

Luigi, looking for Dynamite George under the ore car, stopped abruptly. An eerie sound, familiar from his working days in the Bay tunnels, throbbed around him. His scalp crawled.

"Water and rock are breaking through somewhere!" he screamed. He ran to the engine and quickly started the train. "We gotta make a run for it!"

Dynamite George sensed imminent danger. In a panic, he sprang onto the engine, landing between Luigi's muddy boots. His wet, furry body quivered in fear as he sought a safe place on the train floor.

Pedro ran down the main tunnel ahead of the ore train. "Flood! It's flooding! Get out!" he screamed to the rest of the men in other drifts.

Luigi frantically pounded the train's horn, and Pedro jumped aboard next to him.

Arnie and Billy, hearing the shouting and urgent blasts of the horn, charged down the drift they'd been working and jumped into an ore car. Grinding the gears, Luigi tried to speed the train forward to the drift where Andy and Woody were drilling.

The train picked up speed and careened toward Andy and Woody's section. They, too, had heard all the yelling and the blasts of the train horn. They tumbled down the incline and jumped into an empty ore car. Grasping his chest, Luigi moved from the engine to an ore car.

"You take over, Andy! My heart!" he yelled.

Andy took the lever and started speeding ahead when booming sounds of crashing rocks and timber terrified the miners and Dynamite George. Cramped in a corner behind all the muddy feet, he bristled and stamped his hind feet in alarm.

Chapter XII
THE MINE IS FLOODING

Andy raced the train down the tracks. He prayed the bouncing ore cars wouldn't derail. Behind them a thunderous, wrenching crash shook the mine. Level Seven became a wind tunnel spewing a muddy spray full of debris over the miners. They looked up at the roof and hoped the metal webbing would hold the rock that was weakening from the earth's vibrations.

Dynamite George felt the train rocking and the water swirling around his body. With a powerful leap he jumped up to safety. He landed on Andy's chest and dug his claws into Andy's neck.

"Aaagh!" Andy yelled above the crashing noise. A beam of light from a cap lamp showed Dynamite George clinging to Andy's slippery wet-gear.

"It's the pack rat from the change room," Andy yelled in surprise. Opening his wet-gear he firmly pushed Dynamite George inside on top of his shoulder.

"We chased him out of the drift!" Luigi yelled.

A wall of thundering water hit the train. "Aaaaay, Lord help us!" Pedro screamed, feeling the water covering his body, "We're gonna drown!" The diesel engine sputtered to a stop.

"Jump! Swim to Drift No. 4!" shrieked Andy. "It's a hundred feet ahead on the left!" He jumped off the crowded engine and was swept away in the strong current. He struggled for his footing in the rising water and grabbed a vent bag held by a cable. Using all his strength, he worked his way along the rib until his light picked out red letters on the rock: No. 4. He let go of the cable and swam toward the entrance of the drift to reach higher ground.

Dynamite George felt the water engulf Andy's wet-gear. He dug his claws through Andy's shirt into his shoulder and felt Andy's muscles ripple and struggle against the current. There was no escape from the water.

Luigi watched Andy's light disappear around the corner into the drift. He cried hoarsely, "I don't think I can make it!"

"We gotta make it. It's our only chance, Luigi. The water is flooding the whole tunnel!" Billy roared from the ore car.

He grabbed Luigi by the shoulders, forcing him to jump with him. They floundered in the torrent as the angry waters whisked them downstream, smashing them against the ribs of the tunnel. They reached out in desperation to grasp the yellow vent bags.

"We're goners," groaned Luigi, hanging onto the bag while the merciless current ripped at his arthritic body.

Ahead of the other miners, Andy swam up drift No. 4 until his feet touched the ground. He scrambled up the incline and was out of the rising water. Fifty feet ahead, he discovered the deserted drift was barricaded with large planks of wood.

At the same moment, he felt movement and heard a weak cough underneath his wet gear. "I forgot about ya, fella." Reaching inside his drenched clothing, he gently checked out Dynamite George. Andy reassured him, "You're gonna be all right, fella. We're gonna make it out of this mess."

Looking down the drift, Andy could see only two cap lamps.

"Two are gone!" Andy yelled, charging back down the drift. Dynamite George flattened his sensitive ears and dug his claws into Andy's shirt as Andy stumbled down the incline.

Luigi, still clinging to the vent bag, slowly worked his way along the rib behind Billy. The water was up to his shoulders, and the raging current was rapidly sapping the little strength left in his arms. In a matter of seconds, the water pulled him under. Luigi's gnarled hand held onto the vent bag, his only link between life and death. Luigi's cap lamp faded. Looking behind him to see what had happened, all Billy could see was a white-knuckled hand gripping the vent bag.

"Luigi's drowning!"

Adrenaline coursed through Billy's body when he saw a mining partner torn away by the torrent.

"Hang on, Luigi!" he screamed above the thundering flood. Battling against the current, he worked his way back until he reached Luigi's hand. He grabbed Luigi by the arm and pulled him tightly to him. Encircling Luigi's body, he shoved him up against the rib, accidentally hitting Luigi's head against the roof of the tunnel. Billy's arms felt like they were being torn out of their sockets from the extra weight of Luigi's semiconscious body. Fighting the strong current, Billy reached for the rusty cable that held the vent bag. It stripped the flesh off his hand.

The others heard him yelling. They turned back to help, plunging into the rising water when they saw lights from two mining hats floating on the surface. Woody and Pedro quickly locked wrists to make a human chain with Arnie who reached out to grab Billy's arm. Billy held Luigi with all the strength in his left arm, as the sinews in his neck snapped. At the same time, he felt as if his right arm was being dislocated by Arnie's unrelenting grip. To the miners' great relief, they saw two heads emerge instead of one. Billy had a bear hold around Luigi's chest.

Andy jumped into the rising water and helped Arnie, Pedro and Woody pull Billy and Luigi out of the torrent. Staggering up the drift, the miners dragged Luigi's semi-conscious body to the barricade. Andy started yanking off the wooden planks and crawled through to the other side and pulled Luigi's body through. Billy was still coughing and sputtering when Arnie shoved him through the hole in the barricade and followed right behind. By the time Woody and Pedro followed them, the water was already lapping at their feet.

"Woody, use CPR on Luigi!" ordered Andy. "Arnie, help me tear down the vent bags to block the rising water!"

Putting pressure on Luigi's chest, Woody started to count: "One, two, three." He took several great gulps of air, held Luigi's nose, and blew into his mouth. Luigi started to cough and sputter out water.

"You sure didn't stay drowned long, Luigi," Woody said with relief.

"Get over here and help with this barricade. The water is breaking through!" Andy shouted. "We don't have much time."

The miners pulled down everything they could find to try and stop the water. But the water continued—-

In desperation, Andy yelled, "Use your wet gear, too." He stripped off his own slicker and there, on his shoulder, trembling and clinging to his shirt, was Dynamite George.

Andy was conscious of sharp toenails digging through his shirt, into his flesh. He hesitated, then put the shivering animal underneath his wool shirt and thermal underwear, close to his skin.

"We gotta get to higher ground before our lights give out," yelled Woody, seeing his light dim to a weak yellow glow.

"Water is pouring through the cracks and weakening our barricade," Andy said while helping Luigi to his feet.

Woody and Arnie slipped their arms around Luigi to help him walk up the drift. Billy, still weak, followed behind.

Dynamite George felt warmer under Andy's wool shirt and thermal underwear. It was easier to balance on Andy's shoulder now that Andy had slowed to a steady plodding pace.

The exhausted miners waded through the rising water in darkness as each cap lamp began to fade. They desperately searched for higher ground to escape the flooding water pouring over the barricade.

"Can't keep going," Luigi gasped, collapsing in Woody and Arnie's arms.

"Don't give up, Luigi," Andy said urgently. "The water's flooding this drift and we gotta find higher ground."

"Andy, help with Luigi," Arnie said. "I know this drift and there are some exploration holes ahead of us. Should be a ladder on the left. I think we can fit into that exploratory hole."

Andy slipped his arm around Luigi's waist while Arnie surged ahead in the rising water.

"The barricade must be totally gone," Andy yelled, as he felt Luigi stagger. "Come on Luigi, you can do it."

"My heart! It's flipping!" Luigi gasped fearfully.

"Pedro, help me with Luigi. He's getting weaker," Andy yelled. "Woody, you go ahead with your cap lamp. The rest of us will turn off our lights to save the batteries."

Lighting the way, Woody pushed through the rising water. Pedro supported Luigi around the waist to help Andy. Andy continued forging ahead like a tank, and his body's heat steamed from the exertion from aiding Luigi. Dynamite George was getting hot. He crawled out from under the wool shirt. His long whiskers tickled Andy's neck.

"You stay put if you wanna get outta here alive, George," Andy said, pushing the pack rat gently back beneath his shirt.

Up ahead they could hear Arnie yelling.

"Come on Luigi. Arnie's found the ladder to the exploratory hole," Pedro said hopefully.

"My heart!" gasped Luigi.

Up ahead they could see a light suspended from above. Then it disappeared and returned, shining down a wooden ladder.

Woody plowed through the rising waist-deep water to the ladder and turned back to the other miners.

"We're almost there, Luigi," Andy yelled.

Being the youngest and strongest, Woody took Luigi's limp body from Andy and Pedro. He placed him on the rung in front of him and helped him up the ladder. Ten feet above the floor, Arnie pulled Luigi into the small excavated area. Woody helped Andy and Pedro up the ladder.

"Come on up, Billy," puffed Andy. Dynamite George could feel Andy's heart pounding from the exertion.

"I can make it," Billy gasped, as he crawled over the top of the ladder into the exploratory hole. Arnie pulled Luigi back into the far end of the cavity to make room for the other miners.

"There's room," assured Arnie as Woody and Pedro squeezed close together to make room for Luigi's stretched out body.

Andy loosened the stricken miner's clothing and took his pulse. "His pulse is weak. Don't know how bad his heart is," he said.

They sat in the hole with their backs against the rock. All of them were breathing hard.

"Do you think he'll make it, Andy?" Woody asked, fearing help wouldn't come in time to save Luigi.

"I've done all I learned in the mine rescue Advanced First Aid class," Andy said, holding Luigi's head in his lap. "If he gets worse, we'll take turns giving him CPR until we are found."

"He's an old sandhog. He went through living hell working underneath the San Francisco Bay on that tunnel," Andy said, his voice cracking with emotion.

Pedro shook his head and wondered if any of them would get out of this alive. He thought of Chiquita, her shiny black hair and flashing eyes. His eyes clouded as he thought of her gentleness toward their children. He never told her how important she was to him. She would love to hear the story about the pack rat getting into her tamales, he chuckled to himself.

"What in tarnation are you laughing at?" asked Billy in amazement.

"That pack rat getting into our lunch buckets. If we didn't chase after him, we would be goners. That bandido saved us," Pedro answered, with a laugh.

All the miners started to laugh and point at each other.

"Yep, he took your bearclaw necklace."

"Your class ring."

"And Luigi's watch."

"My teeth!"

The fear and tension were broken.

"He's breathing easier now," Woody said, as Luigi stirred and his breathing became less labored.

With his long fingers, Andy reached into his shirt, gently encircled Dynamite George and held him in his large hand.

"Luigi, you gotta hang in there. Here's your buddy who stoled your watch and then saved you!" Andy said while shining his cap lamp on the pack rat.

Luigi's eyes fluttered open and a slight smile came to his lips. He tried to raise a hand but he was too weak.

Dynamite George's perky face looked at Luigi and at the other miners. Sensing no danger, he crawled back to Andy's shoulder and started to groom his coat and whiskers.

"Look at that," Woody mused. "Knowing critters, I'd say we're safe or he'd be full of alarm."

"We'd better turn off our lights while we're waiting. Watching the water won't make it go down," Andy advised.

"It won't go down in time to save me," Luigi whispered. He knew if he didn't get help soon, his heart was going to give out.

"We're not under an ocean. Just an underground river or aquifer broke through," Andy reassured Luigi. "The water will empty out into sump. The sump pump will be pumping water out of the mine."

The hours passed slowly. The miners used only one light at a time. Andy and Woody saved their batteries to signal the Eagle Mine Rescue Team when, and if, it arrived. The water receded slowly down the ladder, rung by rung.

The men sat in darkness that had no stars, nothing to resemble light. The air felt heavy, and it was getting hard to breathe.

Luigi was breathing with little gasps. The men started CPR again on him, taking turns as time stood still in the black hole.

"Will he make it?" Billy asked, feeling they were all doomed.

"Don't know," answered Andy in a tired voice. He felt Dynamite George squirm. The thick, heavy air was making all of them sleepy. Andy opened his shirt for Dynamite George to get more air.

"How long do you think we've been here?" Pedro asked, wondering if the Eagle Mine Rescue Team could find them.

"I'm gonna check the water," Woody said, as he crawled over the other miners. He shone his light on the ladder and started to climb down. Slowly he lowered his body into the water and looked straight up. The roof of the drift was high above him.

He climbed back up the ladder, turned off his light, and sat in the dark, thinking.

"They're looking for us. I know it. But they will never find us up here with water in this drift," he said.

He thought of the wild horses he broke and being quarterback of his high school football team. He remembered learning to swim in the icy cold lakes of Montana. "I can do it. I'm tough as nails," he said to himself, "and if I don't do it, we're gonna lose Luigi."

Off came his mining boots, Levi's, wool shirt, and thermal underwear down to his T-shirt and jockey shorts. He tore his shirt into strips to make a headband to tie on his mining hat. He adjusted the mining belt around his waist and slipped the battery around to the small of his back. He was ready.

When Woody snapped his light on, Andy asked, "What do you think you're doing?"

"Going for help," Woody answered, looking at Luigi's ashen face in Andy's lap. A soft smile came to Woody's face when he saw the greatest pack rat thief of all time peeking at him from under Andy's shirt.

"Yer crazy," said Billy, thinking of the icy cold water below. "You'll freeze to death."

"You can't get past the barricade," warned Pedro, trying to discourage Woody.

"I'll go through the hole," Woody said confidently. "The water is going down. It'll be too late for Luigi if we wait."

Andy didn't know what to do. Woody was tough, but what were his chances? If he didn't make it, there would be two of Andy's miners lost, Luigi and Woody.

"You can't stop me," Woody said. "Mick's team is on the way to our workings. It will miss drift No. 4 and the barricade."

"Does anyone on day shift know about this exploratory hole, Arnie?" Andy asked.

"Don't know. We were just following a small vein of ore before they closed down the whole drift. It gave out this summer," Arnie answered. He hoped some of the miners he worked with remembered this drift they had explored.

Woody backed down the ladder. The rough stone of the tunnel walls skinned his bare knees and calves.

Determination was all Woody knew when he entered the freezing water. His hands hit the ribs of the drift as he swam toward the main tunnel. It seemed like forever until he saw the outline of the barricade. He swam to it and held onto the lumber at the top. He rested before he dove underneath, sliding through the large opening. When he came up on the other side, he wondered how much longer he could force his numb body through the water. And worst of all, his light was fading.

If I can just get to the main tunnel, I can work my way toward the station in the dark if I have to, he thought to himself.

The water was receding back down the drift and running into the main tunnel. He felt the current take him toward the station. He turned over on his back and rode the receding water while his light bounced off the roof of the tunnel.

The roof seemed higher now. He turned over and started to swim with the current toward the station, bumping into the fallen vent bags. He struggled as his body tangled in downed cables.

I've gotta make it, was his last thought, before the current pulled him under.

Chapter XIII
MINE RESCUE TEAM

Sirens from the mine shrilled through the still night air. Lights in the mining town snapped on and the Eagle Mine Rescue Team rushed to the fire station.

Mick, captain of the team, yelled, "Where's Skinny Wren?"

"I'm here," answered Skinny Wren, entering the fire station with half of his clothing in his arms.

The five men squeezed into Mick's Ram Charger. Tiny, a large blond Russian, spread his massive body across the front seat. He was the powerhouse of the team. Ferret, a small muscular man, sat in the back seat with Skinny Wren and Sonny Jones. In emergencies, Ferret was known for his quick decisions and actions. He could also squeeze through small openings. Skinny Wren, the old-timer of the team, knew rock and had a sixth sense about the underground world. Sonny Jones was a trained Emergency Medical Technician. The team was ready for action as they sped across the desert floor to the base of Sheep Mountain.

Pickups from the town followed them on the road. Two vehicles, one containing Pedro's family and the other Luigi's, was already waiting at the foot of the mountain.

The Bassett family followed the other vehicles in their old van. Melanie Anne, ashen-faced with fear, sat in the front seat. The piercing sounds of the sirens penetrated the van. She thought of all the coal miners she knew who had died in mining accidents.

"Ma, don't worry, this ain't a coal mine. Won't be no methane gas or explosions," Ned said, looking at his mother's pinched white face.

"Pa's tough! He'll make it, Ma," Ted said, trying to calm her fears. Windy, in the back, wished Jamie and Grandpa Lee were with them. She tried to calm her sobbing younger sister and wrapped her in the blankets her mother had brought from the trailer.

In the Ram Charger, Mick was grumbling about how slick the road was and the trouble the Cadillac ambulance would have driving down the mountain if they needed it. He hoped the flight-for-life helicopter in Casper had been notified. At the edge of his mind, he rehearsed all the hours of training in mine rescue and hoped it would be enough to save the miners.

His anger at the mining corporation spewed out in curses as he thought how management forced them to mine Level Seven under poor conditions. The company was so cheap they wouldn't send the Eagle Mine Rescue Team to the Mining Academy for advanced training. Management said it wasn't necessary in their safe mine. Mick slipped back and forth between anger and fear while he thought about each piece of rescue equipment stored in the mining office.

Mining is safer now, but it's still one of the most hazardous jobs in the world, he thought to himself.

The men of the Eagle Mine Rescue Team talked about Level Seven. "Must have hit an aquifer or underground river," said Sonny.

Level Seven had given Sonny the creeps. When they needed a heavy equipment operator for the snow plow, he chose the lower pay, giving up his gypo bonus.

"Is Joe Sheepshead on his way up?" asked Skinny Wren.

"First person I called after you. He is trained for this type of emergency," Mick answered, knowing Joe was the most experienced hoistman in Wyoming. If anyone could talk that cage up from the mine, the old Navajo could.

"Looks like a funeral already with all those pickups behind us," Skinny Wren said. "Level Seven's been full of Tommy Knocker noises, and that greenhorn geologist said it was nothing."

"Stop it!" Mick growled. "Gilbert didn't know any more than we did about where those noises were coming from. Who knows what we're up against. Don't you start talking about superstitions and Tommy Knockers."

The Ram Charger passed through the chain-link fence gate and skidded to a stop in front of the mining office. The mechanics were waiting inside for the Eagle team.

"Level Seven is flooded!" Harry the Mole yelled.

"Jim hasn't been able to get the cage up," Manny the welder said tensely. "Electrical is down and we think it shorted out."

"Turn off those dang-blasted sirens," Mick ordered. "And find Sparkie, and get him here. We need to get that cage up."

"I'm here now," Sparkie the electrician answered. "Had trouble getting past all the trucks, coming up the mountain."

"Find out why the cage is shorted out," demanded Mick. "And, Joe, you take over the hoist."

"On my way," said Joe at the door.

These men at the Eagle Mine were one of the many mine rescue teams in the country. Each man was trained in special areas of rescue in mining accidents.

Mick looked through the window at the mining families crowded near the top of the shaft. He and his team hurried to dress in their diggers, boots, mining hats, and cap lamps.

Next came the mine rescue gear. They slipped into their harnesses and shouldered forty-pound, self-contained breathing tanks full of oxygen. Sonny picked up extra waterproof packs full of first aid equipment and dragger tubes to test for dangerous gases.

Mick knew that if the electrical system was shorted out, the vent bags were down too. Without fresh air, the radon gas would be high. Other packs containing wrenches, wire cutters, screwdrivers and axes were hooked to their belts. Finally, Mick grabbed the bright orange nylon rope from the office wall. The rope would link the team together underground.

The Eagle Mine Rescue Team was ready to go. They walked over to the mine shaft to wait for the cage.

Sparkie was familiar with the transformer and he rerouted the electricity to the cage's electrical box so it could be raised.

Joe slowly brought up the submerged cage. When it appeared, they put on their masks, looking like spacemen ready to step onto the moon. Everyone crowded around the cage when it arrived. Pedro's wife, Chiquita, started to howl when she saw the cage full of debris but no miners.

"They've drowned!" she screamed.

Before Mick put on his breathing mask, he tried to comfort the mining families. "Don't worry. They're safe. They went to higher ground and we'll find them," he said, wishing all the while that he really believed his own words.

The rescuers were all hooked together to the bright orange rope. "Okay men, think positive that we will find them," Mick said, trying to keep the rescuers focused. "We can't make any mistakes. And we don't know how bad the flood is."

They wrenched open the door to the cage, removed broken timber from the floor, got in and secured the latch. They pulled out their Draeger tubes so they could check the air. Mick signaled for Joe to lower the cage cautiously to Level Six. Joe was very tense as his hands gripped the handles of the gears that lowered the cage.

The team was silent as they descended down the deep shaft through the choking mist.

They stopped at the Level Six Station and they got out of the cage. They checked the air then worked their way over to the rusty safety ladders bolted into the rock of the shaft. The air became thicker with moisture as they climbed down the shaft toward Level Seven. Mick, who was first in line, gave signals by jerking the rope. He would check the air with a Draeger tube to see that it was safe and then jerk the rope to continue down. Near the bottom his cap lamp reflected off the water below.

"Looks like a dang river in the tunnel," he shouted up the ladder. Above him Skinny Wren looked down.

"No way they could have made it through that flood," Skinny Wren answered dismally.

Through the thick heavy air, they could see the water was still flowing.

"We'll go down to the water level and wait. Looks like the water on this end is draining into the sump," Mick said as they worked their way down to the flowing water.

Mick ordered the team to be quiet. They hung on the ladders, suspended in darkness, and tried to hear signs of life above the sound of the water.

"Anybody down here?" Mick yelled through his mask.

There was no reply. Just the sounds of water, creaking timbers and falling debris echoing through the mine tunnels.

Every few minutes Mick called into the darkness. He was losing hope. He was afraid to look down at the receding water. The bodies would show up in the shallow water, toward the sump, he thought to himself.

It seemed like an eternity before the sound of rushing water quieted. The minds of the rescuers were filled with fears of what they might find.

Mick said, "Water's gone down. I'll see how deep it is."

The team climbed down the ladder. As Mick stepped into the flowing water, he touched the ground with one foot and felt the force of the current pulling him from the ladder.

"It's still too strong," he said in surprise. "We'll wait a few more minutes and see if more of it drains out."

After what seemed like forever, Mick and the team entered the water up to their thighs. The rescuers headed west in the tunnel where the nightshift had last been working. The train tracks were slippery and hard for the team to keep their balance. They worked their way through downed vent bags, compressor lines and cables.

"No way they could've escaped this," Skinny Wren said, looking at the damage the flood caused.

"Stop it!" Mick answered angrily. "We don't have time to think of them as goners."

Farther down the tunnel the water deepened.

"The floor is deeper in the west tunnel," Mick said, "We may get into water over our heads."

"Water won't hurt us," answered Tiny, encouraging Mick to go forward.

Minutes turned into hours as they waded and picked their way through fallen debris. Tiny used his great strength to lift and remove timbers and vent bags from blocking their way. Mick and Sonny shifted the first aid equipment high onto their shoulders when the team pushed ahead into waist-deep water.

"These old bones ain't ready for an underground swimming party," complained Skinny Wren.

"If you aren't tough enough, Skinny," teased Mick, trying to lighten the seriousness of the situation, "we'll just have to find a younger man."

The deep water felt heavy against their bodies as they pushed ahead.

Mick called a halt. The floor of the tunnel was slanting down and the water was too deep for them to continue. There was no sign of the miners, their hats, or diggers. Where could they be?

He looked at his watch. It was 6:00 a.m. and the rescuers had been inside the mine since 4:30 a.m. The accident occurred around 3:00 a.m. Could the trapped miners survive that long?

His team was exhausted from fighting against the current. They held on to some downed air lines and waited. Hoping the water would go down, the rescuers turned off their lights and rested. Heavy breathing echoed off the water and walls.

"What's that?" Ferret asked, hearing a faint sound.

The men held their breath. They barely heard it.

Mick peered in the direction of the sound but saw only darkness. He turned his cap lamp on and yelled, "Is anyone there?" No answer.

"Can you hear us?" boomed Tiny in his bass voice.

They listened. A weak human voice echoed through the pitch black tunnel and they clearly heard someone say, "Help!"

"Who's a good swimmer?" asked Mick.

"I am," answered Sonny.

"I'm not a good swimmer, but I am strong," Tiny volunteered.

"What about you, Ferret?" asked Mick.

"Water and me get along in a shower and that's it," Ferret answered glumly.

Mick took out his Draeger tubes and checked the air.

"We're a little low on oxygen but you can make it without the tanks. Leave your gear here and tie yourselves together," Mick instructed Sonny and Tiny.

They took off everything except their thermal underwear.

They put on their belts which contained the battery packs for their cap lamps and adjusted their mining hats to fit tightly on their heads.

"I'll go back for more help," Ferret said.

"Better wait," Mick advised. "Got to work in pairs."

Sonny and Tiny started up the tunnel. They swam when they had to and pulled their way forward on the downed cables.

Tiny's bulk strength was giving out. He knew he had to reach the man who needed help--soon. Sonny's dim light flashed ahead, reflecting off the water.

"I'm here," a weak voice came from the darkness. Adrenaline pumped through Tiny's veins and he felt his second wind. He started plowing through the water and yelling, "We're coming!"

"Better slow down," warned Sonny. "We don't know how far ahead he is."

Steadily they worked their way forward. Sonny's cap lamp showed one of the many downed yellow vent bags.

"Help, I'm here," Woody said in a hoarse whisper.

Tiny pushed through the water to Woody, who had his arms wrapped around a vent bag.

"We found one of them," Tiny shouted into the darkness.

"Knew you'd come. Luigi's bad off," Woody gasped before he passed out from hypothermia.

"Tie him around me, Sonny," said Tiny.

He slipped underneath Woody's semiconscious body, lifting him onto his back. Woody felt like an ice cube.

"Keep his head high," Tiny said, feeling Woody's head fall sideways. Sonny fashioned the bottom part of the rope into a cradle so Woody wouldn't slip down.

"His head is out of the water," Sonny said, as he finished tying Woody securely to Tiny.

Tiny put his arms around Woody's legs and pushed through the water. Slowly they moved back down the tunnel toward Mick and the other men. Watching the specks of lights bobbing in the tunnel, Mick thought time stood still.

"Stay by the equipment," Mick ordered Skinny Wren as he moved forward toward Tiny and Sonny to help.

"We'll get him to higher ground and try to bring him around," Mick said. "Sonny, open up the first-aid kit and find the ammonia capsules. He's probably in hypothermia and we need to get him warm. We also better find some timber so we can float Woody out."

Sonny opened the bag with the first-aid kit and found the small glass vials of ammonia.

"We've got to try to get him warm," Sonny said.

He broke the ammonia capsule and passed it under Woody's nose. Woody's head moved slightly.

The rescue team started to rub Woody's body with their hands and his white skin started to show a light pink.

Ferret had moved ahead in the water to look for pieces of lumber. He remembered there was a wooden powder magazine somewhere in this part of the tunnel. If they could find the magazine, he thought, they could make a raft out of the lid.

Taking the ax off his belt, Ferret edged along the tunnel in search of the magazine. By the numbers spray-painted on the rib, he knew that the magazine was on his right side. He worked his way along the rib until his legs bumped into the wooden box.

He felt for the lock, took the ax and knocked it off. He then tried to tear the lid off but soon realized he wasn't strong enough.

"Tiny, get over here," Ferret hollered. "I found a raft for Woody."

Tiny went over to Ferret and felt under the water. He pulled with all his strength, but the lid wouldn't give.

"Ax those hinges, Ferret."

Ferret pounded the hinges of the wooden magazine while Tiny pulled. Finally the hinges broke off. With a loud grunt, Tiny tore the lid off. It was water-logged but it could still float.

They moved the lid to where Mick and Sonny were working on Woody, and the team lifted him onto the raft.

It was 7:00 a.m.

"Let's take him back to the ladder and get him up to Level Six," ordered Mick. "The Federal Mine Rescue Team should be here soon."

Chapter XIV
DO YOU HAVE YOUR EARS ON?

The sun brightened the sky over the frozen desert as Traitor Jack Campbell raced his government vehicle down the center of the road. He gripped the steering wheel with his left hand while he switched CB channels. He kept his eyes straight ahead, alert for any movement at the side of the road.

Far-off voices drifted through the static on the sound waves.

"Breaker 1.9, do ya have yer ears on?" he called out into the open Wyoming space.

"Yep. Got my ears on. This is Dirty Coyote."

"I'm Jack Campbell. Wonder if you heard anything about the mining accident at Homestead?"

"Been hearing talk out of Lander on the police channel that there's trouble up there. They're missing some miners."

Traitor Jack felt a chill go down his spine. The miners were still missing.

"Where are you?" he asked.

"I'll be out of your range soon. Going into the Wind River Range, and my boosters don't work in the canyons," answered Dirty Coyote.

133

"Keep me posted as long as you can. My call name is Black Jack. You must have some kind of booster to be picking me up beyond Lander," Traitor Jack said.

Dirty Coyote laughed, "I sure do. You a gambler?"

"Nope. One of the names the miners gave me," Traitor Jack chuckled, not giving Dirty Coyote his real nickname, Traitor Jack.

Soon he heard static on the other end.

"I'm fading. Will try to contact someone else before I go into the canyon. I'll ten-four-out now," Dirty Coyote said. The CB crackled and went silent.

Jack switched to another channel. "Does anyone have their ears on? This is Jack Campbell, federal mining inspector, trying to find out about the mine accident at Homestead."

A faint reply came over the airwaves.

"Wyoming State Trooper Armstrong Nelson here. I've just passed Muddy Gap on the way to the mine and heard a flight-for-life helicopter is on its way from Casper."

"Just my luck to lose you," grumbled Traitor Jack as Trooper Nelson's signal faded. Traitor Jack accelerated, gripping the steering wheel until his knuckles were white.

Did Mick go underground searching for the miners, Jack wondered? Thoughts raced through his mind. Of all the miners he knew, Mick was the best man when it came to mine rescue. But could they rescue the miners when there was a flood? What in the world happened? During his last inspection, he found the operation was up to Mine Safety and Health (MSHA) regulations. Water wasn't unusual in Wyoming mines. There were many underground water tables and aquifers.

Hearing a faint call from Trooper Nelson on the CB, Traitor Jack turned the squelch knob to hear what the officer was saying, but the static was too great.

He looked up from the CB just in time to see a herd of antelope scattering off to the sides of the road.

"Whew, that was too close," he thought as he slowed down to eighty miles per hour.

He thought back to the emergency call from Denver at 4:30 that morning. The Rocky Mountain supervisor said the Eagle Mine was flooding and men were trapped underground. The Federal Mine Rescue Team was flying from Denver and should arrive sometime between 9:00 or 10:00 a.m. Could he get there earlier to help Mick Kelly and his team? Traitor Jack hoped the MSHA Federal Mine Rescue Team wouldn't get there too late.

Hoist Operator

Chapter XV
RESCUED

Traitor Jack sped past the landing strip at Homestead where a snowplow and grader were smoothing out the snow on the runway. He drove through the empty town and raced up Sheep Mountain to the mine. Vehicles were scattered everywhere at the site. Groups of miners' families stood in the cold, talking and staring at the mineshaft. Snow glistened in the early morning sun, and steam rose from the parked vehicles.

"Have you heard anything?" Traitor Jack asked, looking for the mine superintendent in the office. "Where's Harry Groves?"

"He is out by the shaft," Lorraine answered with a sad shake of her head. "I'm on the phone with Denver. The MSHA Mine Rescue Team will be here soon."

"Don't worry. Mick knows what he's doing and he will find the miners," Jack said, trying to ease her fears.

"We haven't heard a word since they went underground around 4:00 o'clock this morning," Lorraine answered in a tense voice.

"Takes time to locate the miners, especially if that level is flooded," Traitor Jack answered.

Harry came over from the mine shaft after reassuring the families they would find the miners.

"What do you hear?" Traitor Jack asked.

"No word from Mick," Harry said with tight lips. "But the federal team should be here soon since they are flying here in the MSHA Cessna."

"I'm going to put on my gear and go down to take a look before the federal team arrives," Traitor Jack said.

They walked out into the bright sun, and the mining families crowded around them. Jack took his gear out of his green government-issued Bronco and went to the change room. After gearing up, he entered the cage, his whole body tense, as he thought about what he might find below.

The mining office phone rang and Lorraine quickly picked it up. She ran outside and told Harry, "The federal rescue team has landed. They're on their way up."

"Let's clear this area," Harry ordered. "Tell the men to move all the trucks and cars and park off the road by the fence below the mine. We'll need room for the flight-for-life helicopter and rescue team. And get the kids away from the shaft and landing area."

"No way am I going to leave the shaft when my dad is down there," Mick's son Danny asserted stubbornly.

"We're not moving an inch while my dad is missing," Pedro's daughter Angie sobbed.

"You have to make room for the flight-for-life helicopter to land," Harry answered above all the protests. "Move down by the fence so you will be safe."

"Lorraine," Harry said, "call the Broken Spoke for coffee, hot chocolate, and sandwiches to be delivered to the mine."

A Consolidated Ores company van stopped at the mining office. The five members of the MSHA Mine Rescue Team jumped out. They wore coveralls with red, white and blue emblems on the left pocket. The team exuded confidence as they unloaded their gear. Their white mining hats glistened in the morning sun.

Harry and Sparkie went over to the federal team at their van.

"The transformers are cut off on Level Seven," assured Sparkie. "Anything else you think we should shut down, just let me know."

"We have to talk to the mining inspector who is already here. Where is he?" inquired the captain of the team.

"You mean Jack Campbell. He's gone down into the mine to check out the conditions before you guys arrived," answered Harry.

Wyatt, the night watchman, drove up in his white Jeep Wagoneer with its large Wyoming "Search and Rescue" emblems on the doors. He stopped and parked next to the van. Two young men dressed in heavy down parkas got out, looking tensely around at the anxious faces.

"Here are the scuba divers," Wyatt announced as they took a deflated raft, wet suits and scuba gear from the back of the Wagoneer.

The hoist house bell rang: a signal from Level Six. Traitor Jack was ready to come up.

He arrived topside with Jake, one of the mechanics who was working on pumping the water out of Level Seven. He went over to Harry and the MSHA team to report that the water was slowly receding. "The water's going down but trying to empty it out with one pump in the sump is like trying to empty the ocean," Traitor Jack said with discouragement.

The group crowded into the conference room to look at the map of the mine. Harry placed his finger on Level Seven in the west tunnel. "That's where they were working. We got into some poor ground but the geologist's drill samples and exploration didn't show us there was an underground river."

"The old-timers were talking about Tommy Knockers on Level Seven," said Traitor Jack. "When I did my last inspection, the water table was seeping and flowing through the ribs and roof. But that's normal for this region. These mines are known for being wet." There were no safety violations on Level Seven, but Traitor Jack felt guilty for not finding a weakness. He prided himself on his instincts in finding weak rock underground.

"Could be on a fault. We'd need a giant X-ray machine to know exactly what is happening to the earth," Harry said. He was determined to mine Level Seven no matter how wet and deep the water was. Consolidated Ores had to meet their quota and Level Seven contained the highest grade uranium ore in the mine.

"We hope Mick's team has found them by now. The workings were in the west tunnel where we think the flood started. If not, we're in for a long day," warned Traitor Jack.

"We're ready—no matter how long it takes to find them," snapped the captain of the federal team. He finished studying the mine map, folded his notes and sketches, and put them into a waterproof pouch. The two scuba divers sat patiently waiting to be summoned if they were needed.

The federal team put on their breathing apparatus and packed up the mine rescue equipment.

Jake came into the conference room. "It looks like the Colorado River is flooding on Level Seven. The sump pump isn't enough. So I put another pump on Level Six with hoses reaching down to Level Seven. I'm up here to get more pumps and hoses to pump the water out to the surface," Jake said.

"How deep is the water on Level Seven?" one of the rescuers asked.

"I'd say 'bout knee- to waist-deep and still flooding. The extra pumps should help lower the water in Level Seven," Jake answered.

"Let's go, men. We're wasting time, and time means lives," the federal captain barked.

The miners' families and local townspeople waited by the entrance gate of the mine. They watched the federal team enter the cage. The 11:00 o'clock sun overhead was brilliant in the clear blue sky. As the men crowded into the cage, they tried not to bump each other with their equipment.

The damp cold air whooshed up. As the team descended into the darkness, they turned on their cap lamps. They were silent, not knowing what was ahead. The cage stopped on Level Six where the extra pump was working to draw water from Level Seven, 900 feet below the surface.

The federal rescuers descended the ladder to Level Seven, knowing that if the water was too deep, there were two scuba divers waiting on the surface to help.

The team knew that all the escape route ladders in the ventilating shafts were inundated on Level Seven. As a team, they waded through the hip-deep water in the west tunnel in hopes of finding Mick's team. The federal team rounded a bend and could see cap lamps moving slowly toward them.

"Did you find them?" asked the team captain.

"Only found one and he passed out when we reached him," answered Mick in a fatigued voice. "He's going into hypothermia. We've got to get him to the surface for medical help."

"What a stretcher," said the captain as they helped Mick's team pull Woody off the wooden door from the powder magazine.

"Find the wire stretcher by the transformers for Woody," Mick said pointing down the tunnel.

Two of the federal team hurried back toward the transformers for the stretcher. They removed it from the rib.

"Wrap him up and strap him in," ordered the captain.

The two teams helped Woody onto the stretcher. They wrapped him in the wet wool blankets and secured him with straps in order to carry him up the ladder to Level Six.

The federal team's Emergency Medical Technician (EMT) took a small glass vial of ammonia and broke it under Woody's nose. He coughed and shivered. He looked at the faces under the cap lamps and knew he had made it.

"It was flooding. We went to Drift #4, an old workings, and through a barricade. The water was rising. We tried to outrun the flood and the only thing that saved us was a ladder to an old exploration hole," he mumbled. "The drift runs north from the west tunnel."

"Are the others still there?" questioned Mick.

"Yes, and hurry," Woody answered through chattering teeth. "Luigi's bad off. His heart's going."

"Let's go, men," Mick said in hope.

"No. You take Woody up and we'll find them," said the federal captain. "Your team is exhausted. You prepared the way for us by cutting off the transformers and finding where the miners are trapped."

Mick bristled at the captain's terse instructions, but he was exhausted and he knew the families were waiting above for the good news.

Dynamite George was perched on Andy's shoulder. The pack rat listened to Luigi's labored breathing and to the distant sounds in the mine. The oxygen-starved air was thick with a muddy mist, making it hard for all of them to breathe.

Only Arnie's eyes were open while the other men slumbered from exhaustion. He stared into the tarry blackness and listened.

He wondered if Woody had made it. He heard the gurgling of the receding water and Luigi's breathing. He felt Billy squirm for a more comfortable position.

Strange Bilagáana from the hills, he thought. That skinny hillbilly sure hung onto Luigi in the flood. Under all that noise, was a man who shared his passion for life. And those coon hounds Billy brought with him from West Virginia were the smartest dogs he had ever known.

If we get out of here, I'll do better by Billy, Arnie promised himself.

He thought about Dynamite George. He couldn't wait to tell everyone at his Navajo Reservation chapter house the story about that pack rat. It'll top any coyote tales.

But in the liquid darkness, fear nagged at the edge of his soul— fear that he would never see the vast distances of his homeland again.

A loud crack and splash echoed in the tunnel. Dynamite George shot out from under Andy's shirt and landed on Billy. The pack rat stood on Billy's rib cage with one foot poised to run, twitching his long whiskers and fanning out his ears. The noise stopped. Accustomed to the total darkness, he scampered back to his perch on Andy's shoulder.

Luigi started coughing and gasping for air. Frightened at the sound, Pedro started to say Hail Mary's for Luigi.

"Pray silently, Pedro," Andy warned. "Our air is getting bad in this hole."

Dynamite George's sensitive ears picked up a sloshing sound in the tunnel. He scampered to the top of the ladder and froze, listening to new sounds in the mine. He twitched his whiskers, sensing the air for vibrations.

Andy turned on his weak cap lamp and watched the small animal's actions.

"George hears something," he said hopefully. All the miners watched the pack rat in the dull light and concentrated on listening.

"They're coming," Arnie said, sighing with relief.

"Can't hear a thing," Pedro complained.

A little later, they all heard a distant echoing call.

Andy crawled over to the top of the ladder beside the pack rat and yelled down the hole with all his strength. "We're in an exploration hole above the old workings. Hurry! We have a man down."

The sounds of the mine rescue team magnified as they approached through the hip-deep water.

Out of the blackness, bright cap lamps zigzagged on the surface of the water, as the rescuers steadily approached the feeble voices of the trapped miners. Andy's weak cap lamp shining above the ladder was easy to locate.

"Luigi needs help or he's not going to make it," Andy warned as he and Arnie gently lowered the stricken man to the federal team.

Their EMT strapped a small oxygen mask over Luigi's face. The team wrapped him in blankets and placed him in the wire stretcher they'd carried from the west tunnel into Drift #4. They placed the small oxygen tank next to him. They reassured Andy, Billy, and Arnie that paramedics and a flight-for-life helicopter would be waiting topside for Luigi.

The EMT and another rescuer hoisted the stretcher to their shoulders. They pushed through the water toward the main tunnel at a fast pace. Luigi was carried up to Level Six to the cage.

The other two federal men stayed with the miners to help them through the water.

Andy felt light-headed and stumbled. A rescuer grabbed him by the arm to steady him.

"Watch out for the pack rat," Andy said protectively.

"Pack rat?" asked the federal man.

Andy gently pulled the trembling pack rat from under his shirt.

The federal rescuer's cap lamp spotlighted a small pointed face framed by long searching whiskers, protruding black eyes and paper thin pink ears.

"It's a pack rat!" he exclaimed.

"Weren't for that thieving critter, we'd all be dead," Billy said with a strange smile on his tired face.

"He warned us of the water breaking through," Pedro added, his voice quiet with reverence for the small animal.

"Unbelievable!"

"How did he get nine hundred feet underground?" the federal man wanted to know.

"Like any good pack rat, he followed the smell of our lunch buckets," Pedro said with a chuckle.

Billy told the federal men stories of Dynamite George's raids and gave them a pink-gummed smile, saying, "He got my uppers, too!"

Laughter echoed through the tunnels of the flooded mine.

Dynamite George clutched Andy's shirt with his sharp toenails. His ears trembled at the men's loud laughter. His button nose wiggled, sniffing the changes in the air as they climbed the ladder to Level Six. They went to the cage, pulled the chain and waited.

The air became fresh again as they ascended the shaft. Dynamite George could see daylight straight above. His sensitive nocturnal eyes blinked as the bright sunlight streamed down into the cage.

As it jolted to a stop and the gate opened, Dynamite George crawled deeper into Andy's clothing to hide. Relieved families crowded around the miners—hugging them and crying.

Two MSHA rescuers had already delivered Luigi to the flight-for-life helicopter. While they loaded him into the helicopter, Luigi kept mumbling in a delirium about a pack rat in their lunch buckets.

"Something's wrong. Follow him. Follow him!" Luigi yelled unaware of his family hovering over the stretcher.

"Andy, Luigi kept mumbling about a pack rat underground," Jamie said as he pushed his way through Andy's family. "Is it Dynamite George?"

Andy tried to pull the pack rat out. Only a bushy tail showed. The quivering, frightened animal held on with his sharp toenails.

"I'll get him," Jamie said.

Andy knelt down. Jamie reached under Andy's shirt and spoke softly to Dynamite George as he stroked him behind the ears. Reassured, the pack rat turned and leapt from Andy to Jamie's chest, where he burrowed under Jamie's parka.

Chapter XVI
YOUNG SPIES

The legend of Dynamite George crossed Wyoming like a prairie fire. Children on school buses told a strange story of a pack rat saving miners from an underground flood at the Eagle Mine. On remote ranches, they repeated the tale to their unbelieving parents. The story was so extraordinary that the parents called neighbors and shared it. Ranchers and miners stopped their vehicles in the middle of the road to tell the pack rat story.

The Casper newspaper carried an article about five miners saved in a flood at the Eagle Mine in Homestead. The paper said it was rumored a pack rat alerted the miners to the flood. Is this a legend, folklore or folktale from the old mining days? It is up to the reader to decide.

In the aftermath of the flood, the mining inspectors were not interested in stories about Dynamite George. He was just another pack rat living at a mine site. But the miners shared pack rat stories at the Broken Spoke and the best stories were about their own hero, Dynamite George – the greatest thieving pack rat of all.

Amid all the laughter and light-hearted stories, however, a serious debate was raging about the mine being shut down. MSHA temporarily closed the mine until they finished their inspection. The holidays were approaching and there wouldn't be any bonuses if the investigation didn't end and the mine didn't reopen soon. The federal men were concerned about electrical problems and weak rock. They thoroughly investigated every inch of the mine. The transformers had to be rebuilt and the downed electrical wiring replaced on Level Seven.

A small Piper Navajo plane circled and landed on Homestead's snowy runway. Matthew Remington III, vice president of Consolidated Ores, emerged from the plane. He was accompanied by an attorney and a public relations representative. In spite of Remington's navy blue Armani™ suit and London Fog™ overcoat, he shivered in the brisk icy wind. His Gucci™ loafers slipped on the ice of the runway when he approached mine superintendent Harry Groves.

"Can we still meet our quota for the Edison contract?" he asked, while shaking hands with Harry. "You know winter is the worst time not to meet the demand for nuclear reactor fuel in the Midwest. If we don't deliver on time, there's a chance we'll lose our contract."

"We were on schedule until the flood," Harry replied. "I was concentrating on mining the highest grade ore, but all hell broke loose when we hit an underground river. MSHA has shut down the whole operation until they finish their inspection. Plus the union men are stirring up trouble about mining in dangerous conditions."

The vice president's eyes narrowed in concentration and he turned toward the two men following him. "MSHA shut the mine down, plus the union is causing problems. We need to have the mine back in operation immediately."

The lawyer and the public relations man nodded their heads in unison, knowing Mr. Remington would be a strong opponent to MSHA. Consolidated Ores would pull every string it could in Washington, D.C. to meet its contracts.

The men loaded their luggage into the company's Jeep Wagoneer, and Harry drove them to the executive trailer.

"Where are the inspectors?" queried Mr. Remington.

"At the mine," Harry answered.

"We'll unload our luggage and go up there immediately," ordered the vice president.

"You're not going to the mine in those clothes, are you?" asked Harry in dismay.

Remington gave the superintendent a cold look.

"I have an image to keep as vice president of Consolidated Ores," he answered sharply.

"In case you change your mind, there are new coveralls, long underwear, heavy jackets with hoods, and a collection of boots in various sizes in the closet. Remember, you're going to a Wyoming mine, not to a warm boardroom in Chicago," Harry replied defensively.

The men from Consolidated Ores bundled up as Harry had suggested and he drove them to the mine. Mr. Remington wore his Armani™ suit under the coveralls, still believing he had to make an impression to get an upper hand in the negotiations.

In the mine office, he slipped off his coveralls and straightened his tie. He kept his lined boots on because his feet were freezing.

MSHA Special Investigators from Denver and Traitor Jack, the MSHA regional inspector, sat at the conference table. They were reviewing their notes about the accident when Remington and his representatives walked in.

They all shook hands and sized each other up. Lorraine brought in a tray of fresh coffee and passed steaming mugs to the visitors.

"You know we have a contract to meet with Edison, don't you," stated Mr. Remington frostily, his cold eyes staring at the inspectors.

"I'm reminded hourly by Harry that the mine is behind its quota," the lead investigator answered.

"Then, why did you shut down the whole mine?" asked the lawyer.

"We're checking the whole mine for any electrical problems before you can go back into production. That flood did a lot of damage to the transformers below and above," replied the investigator firmly.

"We have teams of electricians working on the transformers and replacing the downed wiring," assured Harry.

"Not all of the levels are flooded—only Level Seven," Remington interjected. "Can't we work on the upper levels?"

"The mine works as one unit. Until the electrical problems are solved, this mine does not go back into production," was the investigator's final admonishment.

"I'm familiar with this mine as I do their MSHA inspections four times a year," countered Traitor Jack. "This is a good mine with few citations. Management makes sure the Eagle miners are well-trained in safety. Problems we cite are always corrected."

"Where is the geologist that let this flood happen?" questioned Remington, wanting to place blame.

Harry responded, "That water breaking through could have happened any place on this plateau. We hit one giant aquifer and it rushed out like an underground river. Our geologist, Gilbert, is checking for weak rock with MSHA specialists on Level Seven. The electrical inspectors and electricians are checking the wiring to see if we can save any of the transformers. We have other teams of electricians estimating the damage on Level Seven and how much cable and wiring we have to order and replace."

Traitor Jack looked at the men seated around the table. It was going to be a long afternoon of explanations and arguments with these city slickers. Having to negotiate with businessmen whose only concern was production and who lacked knowledge of mining operations, was beyond his patience. He felt at home underground or in the vast open country, but definitely not cooped up with greenhorns around a conference table.

Tension was building in the meetings in the mining office. Mining experts gave their opinions to the Consolidated men and MSHA inspectors. Solutions were not easily found, and it took hours of labor underground to repair the damage the flood had caused.

The children of the miners were more interested in meeting Dynamite George than in what was happening at the mine.

Jamie warned the children that the pack rat had to be kept a secret from the mining inspectors because he didn't want them to find the location of Dynamite George's nest.

For the first time since Jamie's arrival in Homestead, he was one of the boys. Andy's son, Corky, had new respect for the freckled-face boy whose pet had saved his dad.

Smiley and Corky, who were freshmen, walked with Jamie and Windy from the school bus each day. The two stocky tormenters offered friendship since Andy had spoken affectionately of Dynamite George.

"Can you guys help Windy and me spy on the inspectors and see if they talk about Dynamite George?" Jamie asked his new friends.

"You don't have to worry — we're watching the feds for our dads. Our families depend on that mine and no feds are going to close the mine down," Corky vehemently assured him.

"I play the video games at the Broken Spoke in the evenings so I can listen to the inspectors there," Smiley said, full of self-importance.

"The union is meeting with the miners at the fire station," Corky told Jamie. "We need someone to hang around there to see if the miners plan a strike against the mine."

"Grandpa goes to those meetings at night and says the union is demanding better working conditions," Jamie answered. "I'll tag along with Grandpa and see what's going on."

"We also need someone to sneak around those big shots in that fancy trailer," Corky said.

"I'll ask Windy's brothers, Ned and Ted. They can sneak up on that trailer and not be caught," Jamie answered, feeling a part of the gang.

"We'll meet down at the bleachers by the hot dog stand at midnight," Corky instructed.

"Check your watches," Smiley kidded.

The teenagers laughed and split up to go home. If their dads didn't get back to work soon, there wouldn't be much of a Thanksgiving, and worse, no Christmas. The mining families depended on their bonuses. Their greatest fear was that if the mine shut down, they'd have to tramp to find work.

That night Smiley's eyes burned with resentment when he looked up from the video machine and stared at the special investigator who was saying, "This mine should be shut down until we core drill for more samples to see if there is another underground aquifer or river."

"You'd have to shut down all the mines in Wyoming if you're looking for water," answered Traitor Jack, defending the mine.

"It was a freak accident when water broke through that weak rock," another federal inspector said, backing up Traitor Jack.

"Well, it's our responsibility to see that these accidents don't happen," answered the special investigator.

A few blocks away Jamie sat in a corner of the firehouse conference room, listening to the smooth-talking union organizers. The miners were resisting making this a union mine. These western miners were an independent lot. Billy Bassett was saying conditions weren't perfect, but Consolidated Ores paid good wages if a miner wanted to work hard.

"You guys will be telling us how many feet we can long-hole and how many hours we can work and what we can and can't do," complained Andy.

"We work as a unit and that gives us strength to demand better working conditions, wages, hospital care, and retirement," answered the union representative.

"We pay into Social Security and we do get medical insurance at this mine," Woody said. "While I'm still young, I want to drill as many feet and make as much money as I can. I'm strong as an ox and you should see my bonus checks. Couldn't make money like that if the union was telling me what to do."

"Unions are good when there are severe problems," said Lee. "Our worst problem is Wyoming winters and underground water. You can't blame management for the deep freeze we're working in."

The men all laughed, agreeing with Lee Claybourne. The union representatives still thought Consolidated Ores could do more for their employees. Jamie started to get restless in the hot corner. No two people seemed to agree on any one thing. All the miners had different reasons to work independently of the union. And Luigi, who normally would have been the strongest pro-union miner, was still in the hospital with congestive heart failure.

In the meantime, Ned and Ted were crouched in the frozen snow below a window of the executive trailer. They strained to listen to Mr. Remington, who was furious at the citations the federal inspectors had written. The problems had to be fixed before the mine went back into operation. Remington demanded that the miners work 12-hour shifts to repair the mine. Teams would have to clean up the wreckage, replace the electrical systems, and hang new vent bags and cables on Level Seven.

The ore train on Level Seven would need to be replaced. A new one was being shipped from out of state to the mine. Consolidated

Ores ordered truckloads of new equipment, electrical wiring and transformer parts. Large wooden crates were being unloaded at the mine shaft. A team of electrical specialists had been flown in to replace the transformers.

Through the steamy window of the trailer, Ned and Ted heard Mr. Remington on the phone yelling at someone on the other end. "If you want me to get this mine up and running and keep our contract, I wouldn't worry about how I do it. If I want to pay the miners double time, I will."

"If the government just stopped picking on little things, the mine would be back in production in a week and meet its quota," he muttered to the men in the room. He hung up the phone, unaware of the two young men who crouched below the window outside.

"Did you hear that? Double time! They sure ain't mean like the operators in West Virginia," whispered Ned. "All he wants is the mine working and he's willing to pay for it."

"We'll have plenty of work. We can make a lot on twelve-hour shifts with double-time paychecks," answered Ted.

Jamie hiked over to the vacant hot dog stand. The stars were so thick he felt he could reach up and pluck one from the sky. The other boys hurried to the meeting place, shivering from the ten-below-zero temperature.

"All they do is talk," Jamie reported. "No one can make up their minds about anything, and they didn't mention Dynamite George."

"The inspectors are arguing a lot. Some are real hard-nosed about the accident, but they ain't miners. Just specialists," reported Corky. "They didn't say anything about your pack rat."

Ned and Ted bit off chewing tobacco, trying to look older than the other boys. "All the big guys want is to get the mine back into production," said Ned.

"Yeh, they're not out to get us miners, 'cause they're going to start working 12-hour shifts and paying double time," Ted said with authority. "And me and Ned are going to work full time."

"You guys aren't miners. Just Vo-Techs," Smiley challenged.

"Sure we are. We're being trained in school and have been working part time at the mine," Ned answered. "When I can make that kind of money, I ain't going to school."

"When do they start working twelve-hour shifts?" questioned Corky.

"Tomorrow, I guess. That's what the big shot said," answered Ted.

"Dad'll be glad to hear that," Corky said.

"I'm going home. It's like a deep freeze out here," Jamie said, as he walked away from the group. "All I heard was a lot of arguing and nobody making up their minds."

"Double wages will make up their minds fast," Ned and Ted said in unison.

The teenagers disbanded, knowing their lives were secure and their families would still be receiving paychecks.

Funny how fast people change, Jamie thought. One minute they couldn't stop talking about the pack rat, and the next, all they could talk about was their paychecks and how they were going to pay their bills. As he walked home through the cold night, he looked at the blinking light on the mining tower and sighed with relief. His pack rat was safe—for now.

Chapter XVII
EVICTION

Dynamite George slept for days after the mining accident. He nibbled on his collection of hay and dried flowers. When he regained his strength, his instincts drove him back down to the mine despite the crusty snow on his path.

He found the mine eerily quiet. He did not smell soap or diesel fumes in the air. The change room was dark. He crawled through the hole in the eaves and let his eyes adjust. He then scampered across the ceiling beam to the grate.

The false teeth were still there by the fan blades. Dynamite George again tried to get the dentures through the small hole of the melting ice. The teeth did not budge. The ice was soft and easier to chew. He broke off pieces with his front paws. He poked his head into the edges of the hole and again struggled with the uppers. With a sudden jolt, the teeth flew out and fell to the ground in a pile of snow.

Dynamite George shot down the side of the building to the sunken teeth. He grasped them and ran across the road to his path up the mountain. Halfway, he collapsed as the teeth were too cumbersome to carry. His tired jaws gave out. In the creeping light of a new day, he left the teeth in a pile of snow and ran back to his nest.

The town and mine were still in chaos from the mine flood. The mine was shut down until the investigation by MSHA was finished. Grandpa Lee and Jamie made sure Dynamite George had plenty of peanuts but they were secretive about their trips to the explosives magazine.

Trucks rolled into town with new equipment for the mine. Meetings continued to take place and many issues were solved so the mine could go back into operation.

The union gave up on the miners. Quotas and bonuses were more important to the miners than their safety. The miners believed MSHA was enough to slow down production. Remington and his crew left to go back to Chicago the morning Dynamite George carried the false teeth up the mountain.

The weather started to warm up. For a few days, warm Chinook winds from Canada ended the frigid temperatures and the snow started to melt.

Dynamite George was invigorated by the warmer weather. During the thaw, he searched for the missing prize he left in the snow on the mountain. He found the uppers protruding from the snow, gleaming in the hazy quarter moon. He gripped the teeth. With head held high, he carried the prize to his nest. Neatly, he placed the teeth on top of his collection.

Traitor Jack was in his small motel room reviewing citations from the mining accident. He could feel a cold winter wind blowing through the flimsy windows and under the door. He pulled a chair closer to the wall-mounted gas heater to keep warm. From the pressure in his head, he knew another storm was moving in after the thaw.

He was relieved that things were finally settling down. Now that he was finished with the mine flood, he had time to check on a phone complaint about a fire hazard in the explosives magazine. Law required him to check out all complaints. He knew Lee Claybourne kept a perfect operation; no problem there, he thought. Lee was a top demolitions man who never took chances. He stretched and yawned, noting how late it was. He decided, first thing in the morning, he would go up the mountain to check out the complaint about the explosives magazine.

Traitor Jack woke to the buzzing alarm. He frowned when he looked through the frost-covered windows. Late in the night, a storm had blown in. Dawn was dark and gray with the sky spitting a few snow flurries. He pulled his insulated boots over several pairs of wool socks and was glad all he had to do was see Lee Claybourne before going home. It had been a long, hard two weeks.

He entered the smoky air of the Broken Spoke and smiled at big-toothed Flossy Foy. He ordered his usual: ham, eggs, and hash browns.

"Guess yer the only one left?" Flossie noted, slopping a mug of steaming coffee down on the table.

"I'll be back in Green River today. Got one more thing to check out with Lee Claybourne and that shouldn't be any problem."

Flossy froze. If he had to see Lee, she knew someone had squealed about the pack rat nest in the explosives magazine. How could she get word to Lee in time?

Rushing back to the counter, she whispered to a group of night shifters eating breakfast.

"Get 'holt of Lee and let him know that Traitor Jack is on his way up to check out his operation and probably the magazine!"

At the main mining office, Mick picked up the phone.

"You must be joking," he grumbled. "We just finished with the mining accident. This means more trouble. I'll go over and warn Lee that Jack is on his way up."

Harry looked up in alarm when he heard Mick on the phone. He was exhausted from dealing with MSHA inspectors and people from Consolidated Ores.

"What in the world does Jack expect to find in the explosives magazine? The inspectors crawled over every blasted inch of this mine," Harry growled. "I thought Jack left with the other inspectors."

"He has a phone complaint that was called in before the accident," Mick answered, impatient to warn Lee.

The superintendent let out a string of curses, saying that the mine couldn't afford any more citations. Mick left the office knowing everyone was at a breaking point. One more thing might be too much. Snow flecked Mick's face as he hurried toward the aluminum explosives building. As he entered, he saw some of the old-timers huddled around the electric heater.

"Grab yourself some coffee, Mick," Lee gestured toward the black-stained coffee pot. "Bet you're glad all the inspections and troubles are over!"

"Not yet," Mick answered, emptying the coffee pot of its potent brown liquid. "Traitor Jack is on his way up to investigate a complaint about the explosives magazine."

"What!" Lee exclaimed. "He seldom inspects my area. He knows I keep everything in shape. Some lowdown polecat musta told him about that nest!"

"Speaking of Jack, he's driving through the gates now," Mick said, looking through the frosted windows.

"He won't cause us any trouble. I've known him since he was a pup, when he and my Johnnie started mining together," Lee replied, trying to reassure Mick.

"I know he doesn't aim to cause us any trouble. If there was a complaint about the nest, he's gotta follow through with the inspection," Mick answered wearily. "And you know what that means."

The new storm blew snow into the building as Traitor Jack pulled open the door. He noticed Mick's glum expression and Lee Claybourne's face etched with deep wrinkles of worry. Jack's instincts warned him that something was wrong and there might be a problem to solve.

He groaned inwardly, thinking, I haven't been home in two weeks and it's nearly Thanksgiving.

"Looks like we're going to have more snow," Jack said cautiously, looking around the quiet room. "Got a few things to check out before I leave today."

"What's the problem? You guys have been through this mining operation with a fine-toothed comb," Mick grumbled. "Didn't you get enough citations from the flood?"

"Just following through on a complaint," Traitor Jack answered defensively. "It won't be any problem, Lee. You've never had a citation since I've been working as an inspector."

Lee looked away from Jack's eyes and started to make another pot of coffee.

Traitor Jack realized there was something drastically wrong by the actions of Lee, Mick, and the other old-timers who hovered by the heater.

"Lee, it'll just take a few minutes to go up the mountain and check out a complaint about a fire hazard in the explosives magazine," Jack said.

Lee nodded, pulled on his old army overcoat, put on his mining hat and covered his ears with the winter flaps.

Mick, his face red with anger, followed them out to the green government vehicle. As they drove up the icy mountain road through the now thickly falling snow, Lee tried to change Traitor Jack's mind about the inspection.

"Getting pretty slick. That new snow on top of the ice might cause you some trouble," Lee warned.

"Yep, it's gettin' mighty tricky," Mick added.

"Won't take but a minute to check out the magazine area, and the road is still in good shape," Traitor Jack answered, knowing the men were trying to delay the inspection.

When they arrived at the explosives magazine, Lee slowly turned the key in the lock. He swung open the great iron door and looked intensely at Traitor Jack, not knowing what to expect.

Snow swirled into the interior room. Traitor Jack entered, pulled out a flashlight and turned it on. There in the amber glow, stood Dynamite George's great nest. His winter forage of food that Billy had scattered was once again neatly stacked on the overhead oak beams and on the wooden floors against the wall.

Dynamite George poked his sleepy face out of the nest, expecting his peanut treats. Realizing there was a stranger with Lee and Mick, he bolted to the safety of the overhead beams.

Traitor Jack was stunned. With his mouth wide open, he gasped and then blurted, "Oh no, Lee! How could you let this happen?"

"He's Jamie's pet," Lee answered in a defeated voice.

"Oh, no! I thought the pack rat lived in the machine shop," Traitor Jack groaned, knowing the pack rat was the town's hero.

"Dynamite George did warn Luigi and Pedro," Lee said with firmness in his voice.

"But, Lee, his nest is right next to the explosives," Traitor Jack said, his words trailing off in disbelief.

"The explosives are in the cavern behind the wood-lined door, and he never goes in there," Lee explained.

"You know the regulations," choked Traitor Jack, losing control and knowing there would be a battle of wills. "No flammable material within 25 feet of the explosives. And this whole room is filled from floor to roof with the largest fire hazard I have ever seen in an explosives magazine!"

"But he's Jamie's pet! The whole town's got a soft spot in their hearts for this critter," Lee warned, pointing to Dynamite George.

"Jack, you'd best let this one go. The miners really have a thing for Dynamite George since the accident. If you wanna cause trouble, just try and evict that pack rat. He's a legend now," Mick said, trying to reason with Traitor Jack.

"You know I don't want to cause trouble, Mick," Jack answered tensely.

"Then just forget what's up here, Jack. We've been friends for years. Evicting Jamie's pet in the dead of winter takes a mean man. And you're not mean, Jack!" Lee said, thinking Traitor Jack would give in.

"Lee, you got me between a rock and a hard place," Jack answered defensively.

Seeing Traitor Jack weakening, Lee started talking fast. "There isn't any real problem. The explosives are safe. So just forget you ever saw that pack rat."

Dynamite George watched the men cautiously, not understanding that his warm, safe home was in jeopardy. He could smell anger and fear in the men below him.

"Sorry, Lee. The complaint is recorded at the main office. I have to take the necessary action. The pack rat and this mess have to go," Traitor Jack said in an official voice Lee had never heard before.

Mick moved closer to Traitor Jack. "We've been through enough problems these last two weeks. You're adding fuel to the fire evicting a pack rat who just saved six lives."

"You know the regulations. You'll have to move the pack rat immediately," answered Traitor Jack.

"If we have to do it, can we do it this weekend when Jamie can help?" pleaded Lee. "We've got to find a safe place to move him."

"By law, this should be cleaned up before I leave," Traitor Jack said, "but I'll bend the rules 'til this weekend."

"You can bend the rules all the way and say you saw nothing," Mick said in a gruff voice. "The men are short-tempered from all the inspections, and kicking out their favorite pack rat will cause more trouble."

"I'll leave a warning down at the superintendent's office saying this violation must be cleaned up by Monday," Traitor Jack replied. "If not removed, it will be a citation."

"By the time you get them eviction papers delivered back to your office and the government takes action against Dynamite George, he will have died of old age," Lee challenged Traitor Jack.

"Don't count on it, Lee," Traitor Jack warned. "We can't sit on this situation. When you move him, be sure he is far enough away that he won't be returning."

Mick's bear-like shape moved toward Traitor Jack. He'd had enough. They'd almost lost Luigi and here the government was picking on a pack rat.

"Both of you know by law I have to enforce these regulations," Traitor Jack said, trying to cover up the emotion in his voice. He never expected to face such personal complications while being a mining inspector. Many of his friends, including Jamie's dad, had died in mining accidents. All Jack wanted to do was help improve mine safety.

Before he closed and locked the iron door, Lee looked sadly at the perky pack rat.

Silently, the three men left and returned to the mine site.

News of Dynamite George's imminent eviction spread quickly through the town. On his return home from school, Jamie heard the secret of Dynamite George's nest had been discovered through an anonymous phone call. Traitor Jack had inspected the explosives magazine.

Jamie started hiking toward the mine with his thumb out for a ride. Through the falling snow, he saw a large snowplow coming down the road.

The driver was Windy's older brother, Ned. Jamie spluttered out the story, and Ned agreed to take him up the mountain. The snow was blowing at a slant and it was bitter cold when they arrived at the mine. Jamie jumped out of the snowplow. Ned followed him into the explosives building.

"Grandpa! Is it true that Traitor Jack found Dynamite George's nest?" Jamie asked fearfully.

"It's true," his grandfather answered sadly.

"When you were up there, did you look in the nest for Pa's teeth?" asked Ned.

"No. I was too dang mad at Jack to think of any teeth," Lee answered sharply.

"Maybe if we find the teeth, they'll let him stay," Jamie said, hoping for a delay.

"Finding the teeth won't help Dynamite George. He's up against the federal government and their dang regulations," Grandpa Lee answered in defeat.

"But Dynamite George is a hero," cried Jamie. "He saved the miners!"

"We have to move him this weekend, Jamie," his grandfather replied.

Jamie's face turned red with anger, "No way. The miners won't let that happen!"

He stormed out of the explosives building, covered his face from the blowing snow and marched with determination to the mine office. Traitor Jack and Harry Groves looked at the door when they heard Lorraine warn Jamie that he couldn't just walk into the superintendent's office.

Jamie paid no attention. Flushed with outrage, he charged up to Harry's desk. His blue eyes turned black with fury as he confronted the mine superintendent and the federal mining inspector.

"What kinda men are you to throw Dynamite George out in a blizzard!" he choked. "He's not in with the explosives."

"Jamie, you know the nest is against safety regulations," Jack said patiently. "And your grandfather knew it too. He must be getting soft in his old age to let you keep a pack rat in the explosives magazine."

"Lee never told me where the nest was. I assumed it was in a cliff, or the machine shop," Harry added. "Jamie, the whole mountain could have blown sky high with such a fire hazard."

"No way. He was just in the small room. He couldn't get through the wooden door to the explosives," Jamie said, defending his pet.

"Son, we have mining laws to protect people and if you want to read my citation book on fire hazards in an explosives magazine, here it is," said Traitor Jack, handing a small blue book to Jamie.

"I don't need to read your regulations! It's just not fair to pick on a helpless animal in the middle of winter," Jamie retorted.

Lee Claybourne walked into the office and heard Jamie's enraged voice.

"Jamie, let's go home," Grandpa Lee said in a kind voice. "You can't fight the federal government."

"Yes, I can. Wait 'til I tell everyone in school and the town what you've done, Traitor Jack," Jamie warned.

"Jamie, Mick and I know a perfect place to put George and his nest where he'll be safe this winter," his grandfather said, trying to soothe his angry grandson.

"He'll find his way back home, no matter where you put him," answered Jamie.

"Jamie, instead of a citation, I'm giving the mine a warning for the pack rat and his nest to be moved from the explosives magazine," said Jack in an empathic voice. "We don't have to tell when the nest was built. You listen to your grandfather. He's in enough trouble already."

Harry said, "Lee, you should be fired but you are a sentimental old cuss. Jack is doing us a favor by giving us a warning. If I were you, I wouldn't cause trouble at the mine about the pack rat. And that goes for you too, Jamie," he advise.

"We'll move the pack rat this weekend to Old Charley's cabin in Rattlesnake Gulch," Lee assured Harry and Jack.

Jamie was disgusted with his grandfather for giving in so easily. "The miners won't let this happen," he challenged.

"Jamie, don't start more trouble with the miners. They need to get back to work and make their Christmas bonuses. Life is not always what we want. Or fair. We just do the best we can and I'll promise you this: Dynamite George will be safe in that old cabin," his Grandpa Lee assured him.

Hearing the sadness in his grandfather's voice, Jamie gave in. Before he left the mining office, he saw that Harry and Jack both looked tired.

Like a dejected old man, Grandpa Lee moved towards his truck, Clarabelle. On the way down the mountain, Jamie thought maybe life isn't fair.

Everyone looked so gloomy and worn out today.

Chapter XVIII
OLD CHARLEY'S CABIN

The day was cold and overcast when Jamie, Windy, and Mick backed up Clarabelle to the explosives magazine. Grandpa Lee had made a pack rat trap. It was a wooden box with a sliding trap door held up by a long string. The box was filled with soft rags and peanuts.

Jamie tried to hide his teary eyes from Windy. She was sniffing and blowing her nose with her head turned away from the men.

Dynamite George poked his head out of the nest and sniffed. Grandpa Lee placed the wooden trap full of roasted peanuts next to the entrance of the nest. When the aroma drifted from the wooden box, Dynamite George hesitated then examined the trap. Greed soon overcame his caution. The instant his bushy tail disappeared into the box, Grandpa Lee pulled the string. The trap door slid shut with a CLUNK!

Dynamite George leapt straight up and bumped his head. He squeaked furiously, scratched at the corners of the box and gnawed at the door.

"He's killing himself trying to get out," Jamie said, his voice full of concern.

"He'll be all right," his grandfather reassured Jamie. "He's not used to being penned up."

In the bed of the truck, Jamie put the wooden trap and covered it with a tarp. He securely fastened the tarp then went back to help his grandfather and Mick move the nest.

Windy gave Grandpa Lee an accusing look.

"Don't glare at me, Windy. I don't make the rules."

He took the snow shovel and wiggled it under the pack rat nest. When he lifted it, its weight caused it to fall off the shovel.

A flash of pink fell out of the nest to the wooden floor.

"Look!" squealed Windy with excitement, "Pa's teeth."

"He did bring them back," Jamie said with relief.

The tension broke. Mick and Lee laughed until there were tears in their eyes.

Windy carefully picked up the teeth and examined them. She noticed that one front tooth was missing and there were scratches on the pink surface.

"I'll find a way to pay your dad to get his teeth fixed," Jamie said. "He told me because Dynamite George saved the miners' lives, he'd forgive him for taking his teeth."

Lee and Mick placed the nest on a piece of plywood and carefully put it in the back of the pickup. Windy wrapped the false teeth in a tissue and gently put them in her pocket. She helped Jamie gather the pack rat's winter store of food.

They picked up the sticks, small twigs and shiny objects that fell from the nest. Then they put Dynamite George's belongings into large black plastic bags: hay, dried wild flowers, dried mushrooms, lichen, piñon nuts, and peanut shells.

"He gathered enough food for ten pack rats," laughed Windy.

"Instinct keeps critters like him alive, Windy," answered Grandpa Lee. "They gather food all summer to prepare for the long winter months. Pack rats seldom starve."

"Jamie, remember last month when we were watching the prairie dogs? They gathered their hay in great mouthfuls and looked as though they were wearing stiff moustaches," Windy said, thinking how funny they appeared. "Do you think they store as much food as a pack rat?"

"I guess they do," Jamie answered wondering how any one animal could store as much food as Dynamite George.

Old Charley's cabin was located in Rattlesnake Gulch, fifteen miles from the mine. To reach the gulch, they had to turn off onto a muddy track that was the remnant of an old road. Clarabelle bumped and rattled along the track and then descended into an arroyo.

"Be careful, Grandpa," Jamie warned. "His nest will tip over!"

Jamie could see the dark shape of the ancient log cabin built on the east side of the gulch.

"Why did he build his cabin down in a hole?" Windy asked.

"To get out of the Wyoming winds," answered Grandpa Lee. "And by facing the cabin east, it warms up from the early morning sun."

"Good place to put the pack rat," Mick said encouragingly to Jamie and Windy.

"He'll be safe from the spring melt off. The cabin is above flood level," assured Grandpa.

"Floods?" questioned Windy. "We're in the desert."

"When the snow melts in the spring, it has to go somewhere," Grandpa Lee answered, pointing to the dried up stream at the bottom of the arroyo.

Grandpa Lee stopped the truck below the cabin. Jamie was anxious to scout Old Charley's home, which was built in the late forties.

When Jamie entered the cabin with Windy close behind, his heart sank. This was nothing like Dynamite George's safe home in the cozy explosives magazine. Wind had blown snow through the broken windows, and timbers had fallen from the ceiling. Old pots, bottles, mildewed clothing, newspapers and magazines were strewn on the floor. There was an old rusty stove with the stovepipe hanging loose.

"Looks like someone was looking for something," Windy said.

Lee and Mick looked around the ransacked cabin.

"Old Charley worked in gold and silver mines before he prospected for uranium," chuckled Lee.

"Rumor is he had a stash but he died out here in the 50's, not a penny to his name," Mick said.

"Yep. I knew him when I was working in the Gas Hills. He'd come into Lander with his ore samples, hoping he was close to a large uranium deposit. Poor old-timer — running around with his Geiger counter. Every time he heard a tick-tick, he'd make another mining claim. Out here it was all poor deposits, but he was so close. If he'd gone a few miles north and done his prospecting around Sheep Mountain, he would have struck it rich," said Grandpa Lee.

"Did anyone find anything in the cabin?" Jamie asked.

"Lots of geological maps, ore samples, tools, and an old prospector's dying dream," answered his grandfather.

"They found him one summer and he was dried up like a mummy," Mick said, shaking his head. "If he had secrets, they dried up with him."

Jamie was heartsick for his pet. He turned and looked through a gaping window into the cold desert landscape.

"This corner near the old stove is away from the windows," Windy said, trying to cheer up Jamie.

He nodded and followed Mick and his grandfather to the truck. They carried in the large wooden platform with the nest. They placed it in a corner on the floor away from the windows. Jamie and Windy emptied the bags of Dynamite George's winter stores. The two friends piled the hay on the old stove and on top of the rusty bed springs before putting the mushrooms and lichens in cracks and in the floorboards. The piñon nuts, peanuts and shells were placed near the nest.

"He won't make it out here in the middle of nowhere," Jamie sighed.

"Jamie, pack rats have survived in the middle of nowhere for thousands of years. Dynamite George won't starve. Or freeze," reassured Grandpa Lee.

"The coyotes and badgers will be after him. Will his instincts keep him safe?" asked Jamie.

"He'll be safe. To make sure, we brought lumber and plywood to board up the windows and holes. Looks like we should put logs or cement at the bottom of the cabin so coyotes can't dig under," Mick said.

Snow flurries started as Lee and Mick covered the windows with large pieces of plywood, boarded up the cracks in the cabin walls, and put pieces of plywood along the outside foundation.

Jamie returned to the truck for the pack rat. He could hear Dynamite George gnawing and scratching at the wooden trap. He took the box to the entrance of the nest and lifted the trap door. Dynamite George darted out and leapt for a rafter. His eyes sparkled with fury and he stamped his hind feet at the friends below who had betrayed him.

"Here's some fresh peanuts," Jamie said, scattering them around the nest and under the rafter where Dynamite George was perched.

When he heard Jamie's voice, the pack rat chattered his teeth. His whiskers twitched violently.

"Boy, is he mad," Windy said.

"One spoiled pack rat," laughed Mick.

"Don't worry, Jamie, it will take him time to adjust to his new surroundings. But the cabin is now coyote proof," Grandpa Lee added.

"It's snowing harder," Mick said. "We'd better go."

The tools were gathered and put into the truck bed. Jamie went back into the cabin and checked on Dynamite George. He was still on the rafter.

Grandpa Lee locked the cabin. On the way back to town, Windy chattered enthusiastically about the surprise for her Pa: his false teeth with just one tooth missing.

EPILOGUE

Dynamite George was restless and finally came down from the rafter to the peanuts and his nest. The old cabin was full of drafts. With old newspapers and rags, he spent a week chinking all the small cracks between the bark logs. Then he started a thorough investigation of the cabin. He found only a few items: a rusty fork, an old razor and an ice pick, but nothing that glittered.

He extended his search beyond the cabin to investigate a fallen shed. Finding only nails and pieces of wire, he left for another small collapsed structure. He slid underneath the old outhouse boards and found a plank with a large round hole in it. Nailed to the underside of the plank were four rotting leather pouches. Impatiently, he chewed an opening through the leather. Rocks tumbled out of one pouch into a hole.

He jumped in, gripped a rock in his teeth and ran out into the moonlight. He sat on a fallen plank and investigated his find. The marble-sized stone sparkled in the pale moonlight. This was a treasure. Off he scurried, back to his nest, his head held high.

At night, he roamed the area to collect and add to his food the last pieces of hay protruding through the snow. In the collapsed outhouse, he found more shiny stones in another decaying leather pouch.

The night before Thanksgiving, he returned to his nest with a glittering rock the size of man's thumb. It was hard to carry it in his small mouth, and he dropped it in the snow close to the cabin porch.

Keen yellow eyes, hiding under some sagebrush, watched the pack rat struggle with the large stone.

Dynamite George grasped the stone tighter when he heard a quick crunching sound coming towards him. He turned and saw bright yellow eyes, a long nose, pointed ears, and long white teeth framing a red tongue, three feet behind him. With all his might, still holding his prize, he took two leaps to the porch. Dropping the stone, he darted through the crack under the cabin door. The coyote, nipping at Dynamite George's bushy tail, thought he had his prey cornered. The predator slid on the wooden planks against the door. WHAM!

Startled, he sat back on his haunches, dismayed that he had missed his meal. He pushed his long nose and whiskers under the small crack and sniffed. A strong, pack rat scent. He was hungry. He yelped and pawed at the crack. He went over and smelled the stone and savored the scent of the pack rat. He meticulously examined every crack, boarded window, and piece of nailed lumber for a possible entrance into the cabin. But Grandpa Lee had sealed off the old cabin against such predators, and the plywood placed around the foundation made sure a varmint couldn't dig underneath it. Jamie's grandfather knew how to outsmart coyotes.

It was Thanksgiving Day. A light snow fell and Jamie was determined to see Dynamite George before the road to the old cabin became impassable.

"Come on, Grandpa," Jamie persisted. "If we wait, that cow path will be drifted again."

"We've got to be at Mick's at two o'clock for Thanksgiving dinner," his grandfather replied.

"It won't take that long," Jamie said.

"Stop your nagging. You're worse than a squawking crow," Grandpa Lee complained.

"Please," begged Jamie.

"Okay, we'll just go out for a short time and check on him."

"All right! Windy wants to come too."

"You two have been plotting against me again!" said Grandpa Lee affectionately.

The snowflakes were increasing as Clarabelle labored down the streets to the Bassett trailer.

Jamie jumped out and ran up the wooden steps. He knocked on the trailer door for Windy.

"Mercy sakes," Melanie Anne said when she answered the door. "What are you two up to now?"

"We're going out to Old Charley's cabin to see if Dynamite George is okay," he said breathlessly, "and Windy said she wanted to come."

Windy bundled up in her bulky down jacket and slipped by her mother out the door. She gave Jamie and Grandpa a sunny smile.

Billy came out of the kitchen to the steps to hand Jamie a brown paper bag.

"We found some chestnuts at the supermarket in Lander. No self-respectin' pack rat should have Thanksgiving without these," Billy said, with a smile showing off his white teeth.

Billy, his dogs by his heels, followed Windy and Jamie out to the truck.

"Lee, I got my teeth back from the dentist in Lander," Billy said. "Dr. Rachet didn't charge me when he heard how Dynamite George stole them. He said he never laughed so hard in his life."

Melanie Anne called from the trailer door, "Windy, where's your hat?"

"In my pocket," she answered brightly.

"Mr. Claybourne, have Windy back in time for dinner at three and you know you all are welcome too," Melanie Anne said warmly.

"We've been invited to Mick's, but we will have Windy back before two," Grandpa Lee promised.

"If I didn't have to help Annie with the turkey, I'd come out and thank that pack rat again for saving our lives," Billy said with one of his rare chuckles.

Old Clarabelle backfired and huffed down the street toward the empty spaces of the desert.

Snowflakes continued falling as they drove through the barren winter landscape to visit Dynamite George. Around the cabin, paw prints were visible in the fresh snow.

"Looks like a coyote was after Dynamite George," his grandfather said, noting all the prints.

Jamie's throat tightened and his heart pounded. He took the key from his grandfather and unlocked the rickety door. He shoved it open and entered. It was hard to see in the dark cabin.

"George! Dynamite George! We got fresh peanuts and something new called 'chestnuts,'" he called, with a lump in his throat.

Dynamite George's sleepy head poked out of his nest. Jamie sighed, bent down and offered his beloved friend his favorite food: peanuts. Small pink paws greedily grabbed a peanut and then picked up a chestnut and bit into its outer skin. He tore at the soft shell and devoured the sweet meat.

"Boy, is he hungry. Wait 'til I tell Pa how he gobbled down that chestnut," giggled Windy.

Grandpa Lee watched the kids for a moment and then went outside the cabin to see if it was still coyote proof. He saw all the scratch marks on the plywood and in the snow at the base of the cabin. Good thing there's a foot of snow on the frozen ground or that coyote would have dug its way under the cabin, he thought. He checked the boarded windows and pieces of plywood covering the cracks in the logs. The coyote had scratched out Dynamite George's winter-proofing of paper and rags in the smaller cracks.

"That is one hungry coyote," Grandpa Lee said aloud, as he returned to the inside of the cabin.

"Jamie, I'm gonna put more boards over those small outside cracks. Coyote scratches are all over the logs. That's one smart coyote after Dynamite George," Grandpa Lee said on his way to get tools from the truck.

Jamie came out of the cabin onto the porch to help. He felt a crunch under his boot. Looking down, he saw a bright colored stone. What a pack rat treasure, he thought, before he examined it closely in the gray light and saw a golden sparkle.

"Grandpa!" he yelled. "Look at this! It looks like gold!"

Windy and Grandpa crowded around Jamie on the porch.

"Is it fool's gold?" Windy asked, exploding with excitement.

Grandpa Lee held the piece up toward the gray sky, "Well, I'll be danged if it ain't gold. Real GOLD!"

Jamie ran back to the relocated nest. Dynamite George, his stomach full of peanuts, scampered to the rafters and watched. Jamie reached inside the nest and found small yellow chunks of rocks. He pulled out a handful.

IT WAS ALL GOLD.

"Sure enough. Ole Charley was HIGH GRADIN' in the gold mines. Dynamite George musta found his stash," Grandpa Lee said with a chuckle. "And that old fox was pretending he was poor as a beggar."

Jamie pulled out another handful.

"Grandpa! Windy! There's enough gold here to buy a new truck."

"Just a minute, son," his grandfather answered, trying to calm Jamie. "Takes a bigger heap of gold than that to buy a new pickup."

"You can put a down payment on one," Windy chimed in. "Like my brothers did on a truck in Lander until they get their bonus checks at Christmas."

Grandpa Lee's gray eyes sparkled. Maybe—just maybe—there was a lot more of that stash. Thinking of the coyote's determination to reach the pack rat, he told Jamie to pick out a few of the smaller pieces of gold and put them back into Dynamite George's nest.

"That coyote is determined and we don't know where Old Charley's stash is. We don't want Dynamite George running around in this snowstorm looking for his treasures."

Jamie stuffed chunks of gold into his jacket pockets.

"Windy, this has to be our secret—otherwise—the whole town will be out here looking for the gold."

"No way will I tell," she promised.

The snow was falling so heavily Grandpa Lee said it was time to leave the cabin and Dynamite George. To make sure the cabin was coyote proof, Grandpa Lee hammered long nails through the door to the frame and floor.

He left the heads of the nails out an inch so he could pull them up with a claw hammer later. He left a small hole under the door for Dynamite George to run in and out.

"He should be safe now," Grandpa Lee said with satisfaction.

Clarabelle coughed and sputtered when Lee started the engine. The narrow rutted road was filling with snow, and Clarabelle's tires started to spin on the climb out of the gulch. Grandpa Lee shifted the battered truck into low gear. Jamie looked back at the muted gray outline of the cabin through a vertical blanket of snow.

Thanks, Dynamite George. We'll get a new pickup yet, Jamie thought.

His grandfather turned the heater on and it let out a high-pitched squeal of grating metal. "Bearings in the heater are shot," he muttered to himself.

It seems Windy was right. There was just enough gold for a good down payment on a new pickup. That would be Jamie's Christmas present. Now I can retire Clarabelle after all these years of faithful service, Grandpa Lee reflected.

He reached a long arm beyond Windy and tousled his beloved grandson's curly red hair.

"What's up, Grandpa?" Jamie asked, wondering about the big display of affection.

Grandpa Lee's kind whiskered face looked at Jamie and Windy's glowing, happy faces.

"Just thinking. Just thinking," he answered.

Dynamite George scampered around the old cabin to stash a few of the fresh peanuts and chestnuts. He went back to his nest and found most of his treasures missing. He ran up to the eaves and poked his head out of a crack. Snowflakes blew into his face. He went back to his nest and curled into a tight warm ball and slept.

The snow continued to fall and the sky turned a dark gray at twilight. The coyote stood outside its den in the hillside, listening for sounds from the intruders. There was only silence.

He trotted down through the heavy snowfall to the ancient cabin. He sniffed at all the new barricades and scratched at the boards—to no avail.

Dynamite George slowly awoke from a deep sleep when he heard yips and whines coming through the front door. In the dim light, he could see the coyote's wet, black nose sniffing at the bottom of the door. Frightened, he ran up to the beam to safety. His whole body stiffened as he stared at the door and listened to the scratching and growling. Finally, the coyote gave up and trotted back through the snow to his den in the cliff. In the cabin, Dynamite George felt it was safe to return to his nest. He curled up among peanuts, chestnuts, and a few small pieces of gold and fell back to sleep.

THE END

GLOSSARY
AND PHOTOGRAPHS
OF MINING

The photographs below were taken in the 1970's and do not represent the latest advances in mining. This is to give the reader an idea of the underground world Jamie and Windy, and Dynamite George experienced.

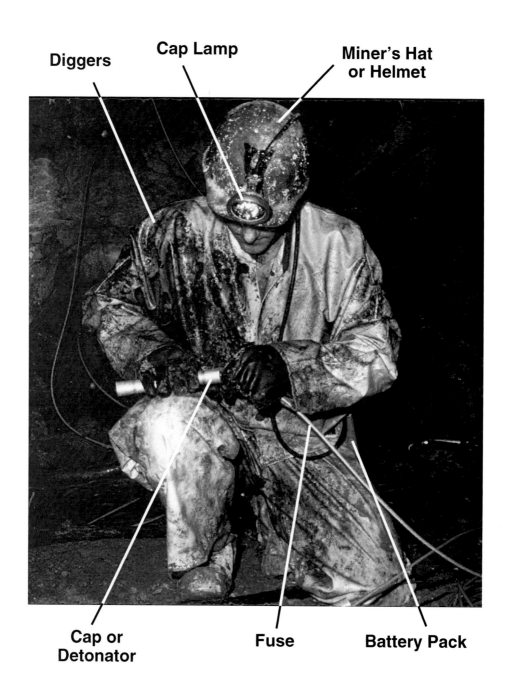

Diggers

Cap Lamp

Miner's Hat or Helmet

Cap or Detonator

Fuse

Battery Pack

Ammonian Nitrate (Prell) - Explosive used in mining and construction: ammonium nitrate and dissolved in water to make liquid nitrogen fertilizer known as urea.

Bilagáana (bilagáana bizaad) – "Anglo person" (white person).

Blasting Cap – A detonator containing a charge of detonating compound, which is ignited by electric current or the spark of a fuse. Used for detonating explosives. See miner photo on page 184.

Cables – Cable that hoists the cage, electric cables.

Cage – Mining term for elevator or lift. The cage transports miners, material and equipment.

Caps – Detonators - A highly sensitive, encapsulated explosive that is used to detonate larger but less sensitive explosives. See miner photo on page 184.

Detonator – Blasting Cap - A device containing a small detonating charge that is used for detonating an explosive, including, but not limited to, blasting caps, exploders, electric detonators, and delay electric blasting caps. See miner photo on page 184.

Drill Bit (diamond or carbide steel drill bit) – A rotary drilling bit that uses diamonds or carbide as the cutting edge.

Drift – A horizontal underground passage off the tunnel which follows a vein of ore. A horizontal passage underground.

Drill Holes – or shot holes – 3 foot holes drilled into a face to put in explosives.

Explosives Magazine – A structure used to store explosives and blasting caps. Prell or ammonian nitrate is an explosive that is stored in this type of structure or inside mountain.

Face – A working place from which the mineral is extracted. The exposed surface of the mineral deposit.

Fault – A break in the continuity of a body of rock. It is accompanied by a movement on one side of the break or the other so that what were once parts of one continuous rock stratum or vein are now separated.

Fuse – fuze, fuses, safety fuses – Your firecracker has a fuse. A cord which contains black powder that burns at a controlled rate. Fuses attach to a blasting cap (called a detonator). See miner photo on page 184.

Geiger Counter – Geiger counters can detect the presence of radiation.

Graveyard Shift – Midnight to dawn.

Ground Water – Water at, and below, the water table; bottom water; below the ground surface; not surface water.

Haulageway – The gangway, entry, or tunnel which mine cars and front end loaders haul ore.

Headframe – The steel or timber frame at the top of a shaft, which carries the sheave or pulley for the hoisting cables, and serves various other purposes. The shaft frame, sheaves, hoisting arrangements, dumping gear, and connected works at top of the shaft.

Hoist – The structure used in a mine shaft for transporting miners and materials. A hoist is also called a cage.

Hoistman – man who operates hoist.

Longholing a face – An underground borehole and blast hole exceeding 10 feet (3 meters) in depth or requiring the use of two or more lengths of drill steel or rods coupled together to attain the desired depth.

Magazine – Any building or portable structure used to store explosives and blasting caps.

MSHA - Mine Safety and Health Administration; (Labor Department) the federal agency which regulates mining health and safety enacted in 1977. See below explanation of the federal law authorizing the United States Department of Labor to protect miners in hard rock and coal mines: The Mine Safety and Health Administration administers provisions of the Federal Mine Safety and Health Act of 1977 and enforces mandatory safety and health standards to eliminate fatal accidents, to reduce the frequency and severity of nonfatal accidents, to minimize health hazards, and to promote improved safety and health conditions in the mining industry. *Public Law 91-173.*

Mine collar – Shaft collars consist of the uppermost portion of the shaft.

Night Shift – Working at night from midnight to dawn.

Powder Monkey – In some metal mines, the person who distributes powder, dynamite, and fuses to the miners at the working faces. Also called blaster helper; powder carrier; powderman helper.

Powder Magazine – A storage area for explosives. A building, compartment, or structure constructed and located for the storage. See Explosives Magazine photo on page 186.

Prell (ammonian nitrate) – "Prell" is a trade name for ANFO which stands for ammonium nitrate and fuel oil. ...It is by far the most widely used explosive metal and hard rock mining and civil construction.

Respirator – Protects miner's lungs from inhaling mining dust.

Roof – ceiling of mine. See roof bolting photo below.

Roof Bolting – metal webbing is bolted into the roof to avoid rock fall. A long steel bolt driven into the roof of underground excavations to support the webbing in the roof. This helps prevent roof falls. Use of roof bolts and metal webs replace lumber.

Self-Contained Self-Rescue Device, SCSR – A self-contained self-rescuer, is a portable oxygen source for providing breathable air when the surrounding atmosphere lacks oxygen or is contaminated with toxic gases, eg. carbon monoxide or fires. Unit contains one hour of oxygen.

Shaft or Mine Shaft – A primary vertical opening through the earth used for ventilation or drainage and/or for hoisting of personnel or materials; connects the surface with underground workings.

Shaft Mine – An underground mine in which the main entry or exit is by means of a vertical shaft.

Shift – The number of hours or the part of any day or night worked.

Stopes – Rooms, made by extracting ore.

Sump – At the bottom of the mine where water collects and the water is pumped out by the means of a pump through a pipe that goes to the top of the shaft.

Tommy Knockers – (folklore) Is a an elf like creature that lives underground in mines. There are many superstitions that date back to the old tin mines in Cornwall about these troublesome creatures. If you hear a Tommy Knocker it is a warning in many mining folktales.

Tunnel – Is dug out from the shaft following the vein of ore.

Vent Bag – Polyurethane bag that carries fresh air down into mine.

Uranium Mining – Is the process of extraction of uranium ore from the ground.

Uranium Ore – ore from which uranium can be extracted.